I0621984

A Letter to Lettuce

Stories and Imaginings

Also by Chris Curtis

Unlikely Tales: Four of the Best
Amazon eBook

Alfred's Tango and Other Unlikely Tales
Short stories

Other published stories in

Blue Crow magazine, Blue Crow Press
Yellow Pearl anthology, Stringybark Stories.
The Village Observer magazine Lane Cove, Sydney
and various other anthologies.

A Letter to Lettuce

Stories and Imaginings

Chris Curtis

A Letter to Lettuce: Stories and Imaginings

First published 2021

Copyright © 2021 Chris Curtis

Published by Palm Garden Publishers
Email: palmgardenpress@optusnet.com.au

Set in 10/12 pt. Garamond

Cover by Palm Garden Publishers

National Library of Australia
Cataloguing-in-Publication data:
Author: Chris Curtis
Title: A Letter to Lettuce: Stories and Imaginings

ISBN-13: 978-0-9872580-2-1

Dedication

This book of fanciful stories and imaginings I dedicate
to my grandchildren James and Sara Martens.
Perhaps I should have called it,
'Memories of the Future Past,' for here there is
something of both. Lives cannot be predicted, but striving
to become the best person possible will create your future.
Let it be full of love and happiness.
To James and Sara with infinite love from Grandad.

Joseph's Coffin

Joseph tapped the sanding block on the benchtop. Wood dust scattered in a busy cloud, wafting luminous in the morning sunlight that streamed through the high glass windows. The sweet scent of freshly milled pine mingled with the familiar smells of varnish and resin. He breathed deeply, smiled and combed his fingers through his greying beard.

His latest project was coming along nicely he thought, almost ready for the first coat of varnish. He stepped back a pace and regarded his work. In the confined space of the workshop, the coffin seemed out of proportion, but he knew it was right.

He had meant it for himself when he began it in the spring, so he knew the length would be more than sufficient.

It would have rested in the rafters until his passing, perhaps for years. Time would not affect the seasoned timbers or plush lining. He would have wrapped it well and it would have waited. Joseph liked everything in its place.

The new plan had changed that, and some alterations needed to be made. The width had needed adjustment of course, for the broader hips. He wiped a wrinkled hand over the lid. A caress. The coffin was his creation, shaped from the rough-barked planks delivered by a tattooed driver and his pimply offsider along the dusty driveway past the cottage. Like Michelangelo, he had taken the coarse wood and released his creation from it. And it was good.

Strange the way happiness can be hunted, sought, pursued but rarely captured for long, he thought. Just when you think you are happy fate intervenes. He was happy for hours at a time but that did not last; there was always an interruption. Sometimes it was the necessities of life but all too often it was she who interrupted.

It had come as a surprise when he realised, he hated his wife. Although 'hate' was perhaps not quite the word. She hadn't done him any harm as far as he could see. He had to admit that much of the fault was in himself. Not that that insight was any help. She represented all the worst things in his life. All the flaws and frustrations. She had witnessed his bitter conflicts and lost battles while appearing to suffer none of the losses that dragged him down like stones. He had put those battles behind him, now he just wanted to get on with his diversions, to pursue the hobbies and interests that he loved.

She wasn't content with her own company. She had no hobbies or interests that he knew of. She rarely read books except for those silly travel magazines with fantasy photos of distant places. All her friends had died or moved away. It was hardly his fault that she could not find fresh interests. Her only routine was the weekly visit to the market, and he could not imagine that was very challenging.

They had been happy once, content with raising the children and making a home. Then the children had grown and moved away. Alice called once in a while. They rarely heard from Mark. At first, they tried to continue as before, tried to maintain the empty rituals of marriage but slowly they seemed to drift away from each other until even the rituals became chores.

He could see that she was frustrated with her life. Joseph understood, even sympathised. He wanted to be happy too, but he would not look for happiness on an ocean liner or in a strange land where no one spoke English and the sun burnt like an open oven. For Joseph, happiness was much closer. He would turn ideas into reality in his workshop.

That was when he realised that his current project was misplaced. The coffin could serve her as well as him. He would be doing her a favour. No more boredom. No more lonely TV nights or pointless meetings of the women's club. He would release her from life and send her to a better place.

She needed to rest from her life of frustration, and he needed a life free of interruption. He made his plans carefully. It was a project worthy of a craftsman. They had spent a lifetime together; he would make sure she would go quickly. He did not want her to suffer, and afterwards, he would ensure that she was comfortable in her rest.

He dipped the brush into the tin and began the first coat of varnish. How would he do it? They still had her father's rifle from the old farm in the linen cupboard, perhaps he could use that? It would be quick. There were a few bullets left, and she kept the gun cleaned and oiled since she had shown Mark how to shoot. The boy was never interested; he had thought it barbaric to kill things. Joseph pushed the thought aside, perhaps he was right but sometimes it was necessary. He returned to the task, drawing the brush in long, careful strokes along the grain of the lid where the wet varnish lay for a moment shining, before sinking into the thirsty wood.

How long had he been at the task now? Weeks? Months? He could not remember. Time crept past in the details of his project. Carpentry, varnish, silk lining; he only had the handles to fit now. He picked up the last of these and felt its texture. Silver with a simple flute. A fine match for the white silk lining.

On the bench, a tray with tea and biscuits. She hadn't said much this time. She seemed to have given up the incessant babble about cruise lines and tropical ports. He was relieved, the constant reminders just made it more difficult. He would make it quick, better to do it in the house. He could blame an intruder while he was in the shed. He would do it tomorrow.

Breakfast was its usual wordless routine. Today was market day, and he could finish his preparation without interruption. He finished his oatmeal and was washing his bowl when he heard the door shut behind her. It was a relief to have her out of the house.

Where was that rifle? It should be in the linen cupboard but there was no sign of it there. He needed to find it before she returned. He would wait until she entered the house and face her in the hallway. It would be cowardly not to say goodbye. He flung open the old roll top desk scattering papers and pens in all directions. It would just make the scene more authentic, he thought. Still nothing. He turned.

She stood in the doorway a frown on her forehead but a smile on her lips. His eyes widened in surprise. She said something that he did not hear. The rifle lay under her arm, her finger on the trigger. She spoke again.

'Bon voyage, darling.'

The Emperor

'**We're** in for a fine procession today, my dear. I really want little Tommy to see this. It's a once in a lifetime opportunity to see our leader in his true persona.'

'Oh, indeed, husband, the kingdom has been sore depressed of late and those executions over the border haven't helped. Even the knighting of Sir Philip has not cheered the people.'

'Well, we can expect a treat today to take our minds off our problems, dear. I understand that the emperor will be bestowing largesse and his cabinet has outfitted him with a brand-new set of clothes for the occasion.'

A cheer rises from the crowd. Horns sound and television cameras swing to point down the dusty road. A brass band starts up. The crowd surges forward.

'I can't see! Get onto my shoulders, Tommy. You'll be able to see our glorious leader in all his splendour. Here he comes now on his white horse. What do you think?'

[Clip clop, clip clop]

'Well, I …… He's not quite what I expected, Daddy.'

'What do you mean?'

'Well, it's a pony really, and it not actually white. More grey really.'

'But what about the emperor, son, what does he look like? Is he handsome and dashing? Does he have a big sword?'

'Mm, not exactly, he is quite a bit shorter than I expected and he has big …. ears, Daddy.'

'Oh, that doesn't matter. What is he wearing? Are his clothes as wonderful as they say?

'Well Daddy, I don't know how to tell you this ....'

'What have I told you about wishy, washy talk, son. Out with it. Be direct, say what you mean!'

'Well Daddy, I don't quite know how to describe his clothes because he isn't wearing any. Just a little pair of red swimmers. I can see his ... er ... . Is he really our glorious emperor?

Father squirms between a tall fat man and a clown wearing a Ronald McDonald costume. Tommy totters on his father's shoulders then regains his balance. His father shouts is amazement.

'It can't be! You're right. No clothes! '

The cheering subsides, confusion spreads, people look at each other. The band stops in mid chord. Silence falls.

[Clip clop, clip clop.]

The old grey pony carrying the small man in red budgie smugglers continues its slow progress. Occasionally, the little emperor dips a hand into bulging saddlebags and casts silver coins to the crowd on either side, his regal head held high. His cabinet follows in single file each in uniform business suit with blue tie. Each smiling his secret smile.

The Message

He enjoyed the wind and spray in his face, the surging power and movement of the ship as it plunged through the night like a wild thing down a dark tunnel. There was no moon but a slight glow in the western sky showed where it might have been. The waves were patterns of dark on darkness felt more than seen as the deck rolled beneath his feet. He drew his thick cloak about his shoulders and stared into the gloom. The ship was running free before the wind.

'You are very thoughtful, young sir, is there any way I can assist you?' Adril turned to greet a short dark man dressed in the fashion of a sailor. High sea boots covered by a long sealskin jacket fastened to the throat.

'No, thank you, Captain. I am simply thinking of my task and I thank you for breaking my mental confusion. Worry achieves nothing but seems to force out all other thoughts.'

'If your task is not a secret, perhaps you could relate some of it to me. We are often short of a good story on a lonely night at sea.' replied the captain.

'There may indeed be a secret', replied the young man, quietly. 'If so, I am as puzzled as any man. I have with me a letter from my father to his cousin the king. I was given no instructions save to take it with all haste to the king personally.'

Save for the soft hiss of water against the ship, the night was quiet. Only the occasional sharp creak of a spar against the mast disturbed the silence.

'Your father, my lord, is a man of great wisdom.' replied the captain', Perhaps, if he has given no other instructions, the message contains all there is to know?'

'Perhaps but would it not be better to advise me on the substance of the message so that I could support it with persuasive arguments and bolster it with clear logic? I am known throughout my father's lands for my debating skill and sharp blade. None can come against me in these, yet I am now rendered mute by the brevity of my orders.'

'Your fame is as widely known as your skill', replied the captain carefully, 'so I cannot answer you. Perhaps then, the answer lies outside the message. Perhaps in the messenger?' Adril turned in the dark to study the other's face but before he could speak, the captain interrupted his intention,

'Forgive me, sir, I must check the helm. There are many sharp snags hereabout, and we must get you, and your message, safe to the king.' with this, he turned and hurried across the deck.

No journey lasts forever, and so it was that the ship and its proud cargo, arrived at last at the port and the palace of the king. Safe on the quayside, Adril called a boy and sent him running to the castle, then waited. In a surprisingly short time, a group of heavily armed horsemen clattered onto the dock, followed by an open carriage. At the head of the contingent rode a tall, lean man wearing a feathered hat and shining bronze breastplate.

'I am captain Sorell of the king's guard,' he said in a stern tone without dismounting. 'I understand that you are Adril, son of Bannock, who is cousin to our king. Is this correct?'

'Yes, it is.', answered Adril formally. 'I have an urgent message for the king from my father. When can I have an audience with his majesty?'

8

'An audience will not be necessary, lord Adril. If you give the message to me, I will see that the king receives it without delay.' replied the horseman impassively.

'My instructions are that I should show it to the king personally.' replied Adril shortly, 'Please conduct me to him at all speed!'

The captain paused,

'Very well, it seems I must bring the messenger as well as the message before the king.' said Sorrel with a wry smile, 'and hope that he is lenient with both of us'.

Adril mounted the carriage, his few belongings were quickly stowed, and a flick of the coachman's whip sent the carriage rattling over the cobblestones and up the narrow streets to the palace. They entered through the main gate, and the carriage stopped before a broad set of stone steps and a strip of blue carpet. Adril dismounted from the carriage and quickly mounted the steps. When he glanced back, the horsemen and Captain Sorrell had disappeared.

'Our guest chambers are this way, sir. If you would follow me.' spoke a small man as he bowed obsequiously.

'Would my lord like some supper before retiring?'

'I need to see the king as soon as possible. Has he been informed of my arrival?' asked Adril shortly.

'The king does not hold audience at this time of night, sir', nodded the servant. 'Tomorrow to be sure, his chamberlain will conduct you to his presence. There is nothing more to be done until that time, my lord. Your bed is ready. Should I bring some supper?' he asked again. Adril clenched his teeth in frustration but managed to reply,

'Yes, bring me supper'. Adding unnecessarily, 'and be as quick as you can'. The butler backed out of the room and shut the door behind him. Adril was not accustomed to being treated like this in the house of his father. He was beginning to have serious misgivings about this assignment.

To his surprise, and the thin straw mattress notwithstanding, Adril slept well and awoke to find bright sunshine streaming through the high windows. He rose, used the available facilities, washed, and dressed. There was nothing more to be done until his audience with the king.

The view through the window revealed the harbour and a garden below. It was a relaxing and pleasant scene and drew Adril's thoughts to his own home and family. A tall wooden door in the garden wall swung suddenly open, and a young girl in a long robe entered. She was carrying a basket and Adril watched as she quickly chose a couple of the blooms, cut the long stems with a small blade, and placed them in her basket. He was immediately impressed. From his distant view, her face appeared sufficiently pleasant, and her shape more than worthy of his attention. Long hair as black as a seahawks wing shone in the morning sunlight. Then she was gone from the garden as quickly as she had appeared. Adril turned from the view; what had been warm and beautiful a moment before was now empty and mundane.

A servant eventually brought some bread and tea for his breakfast and, as he was finishing the last of it, there was a soft knock at the door. He pulled it open quickly and was met with a flurry of sound.

'Good morning, my lord. I hope that you slept well; I am Morden and have the honour to be chamberlain to his majesty the king. I have come to conduct you to his presence so that you can conclude your business here as quickly as possible.' The speaker was a short wide man with a bright smile and brown hair to his shoulders. He was dressed in green and wore a gold chain belt with a small dagger. Perhaps a sign of his office thought Adril distractedly. He decided immediately that he liked Morden so, without delay, Adril gathered up his few possessions and followed the chamberlain as he led him through the castle.

The passages seemed endless but eventually the corridors grew broader and better lit. Adril surmised that they had entered more public areas. At last, they arrived at two ornate wooden doors that opened as they approached. They entered a large, carpeted room. The ceiling was high above them, and the walls were hung with colourful tapestries interrupted at intervals by numerous windows mostly shuttered against the autumn chill. Fires burned in grates on either side and candles lit the darker corners.

Immediately Adril saw the king seated on an ornate throne on a raised dais at the end of the room. He was simply dressed but carried a large sword in its scabbard across his knees. On his head, he wore a crown of gold. Adril's eyes, however, refused to take in more details of the king's appearance as they focused on his companion. The girl that Adril had seen in the garden was seated on a similar throne on the king's left. A simple band of silver encircled her head. She wore a tunic of white with a wide leather belt and silver buckle. There was a moment's silence.

'This is my daughter, Princess Adriana,' said the king with an amused air. 'Was it me that you came to see, young sir? He continued.

'I.......I.......forgive me, my lord.' Said Adril, switching his attention hastily and bowing deeply. He saw now that the king was a large man approaching middle age. His broad face carried a pleasant and amused smile.

'I......My father has sent me to deliver an urgent message and charged me to deliver it to you personally and with all haste, Sire,' continued Adril. He fumbled inside his cloak and finally drew forth a sealed parchment. He handed it hastily to Morden. The chamberlain passed it immediately to the king.

In silence, the king broke the seal and removed the letter within. He looked at Adril carefully.

'I have not had news of your father for many months Adril, and now I have an urgent message. What am I to make of this?' He stared at the parchment in his hand for several long seconds, looked at Adril intently then lifted his eyes to look into the distant corners of the room. Finally, he sighed and addressed Adril with new intensity.

'Do you know what is in this message, Adril?' he asked.

'No Sire', said Adril. He could not think of anything to add.

'Very well,' continued the king leaning back, 'Tell me how your family fairs, what are your fears and hopes for the future. Tell me all and hold nothing back. I wish to know.'

A chair was brought forward, and Adril sat, perplexed by this turn of events but pleased to be asked to talk about his family at court. He began speaking. He told of his father's strength, of his mother's failing health. He told of his sister, Ingrid's marriage to their neighbour, and of the good harvests. He spoke passionately and with pride of his family's achievements, their fears, and their plans for the future. He left to the last the news of the raiders. Surely, this must be the purpose of his father's message. He told the king how each summer they appeared from the north in great ships. How they raided villages and even towns, killing and pillaging. With less sea ice for many seasons now, the raids were increasing. His father's army was small and could not protect all of their lands at the same time. With each sentence, his excitement grew.

The king listened in silence. Finally, when Adril had spent his thoughts, he spoke.

'Good Adril,' he said, 'you have fairly painted for me a picture of your father's lands and all that transpires there. What message do you think your father has for me?'

'I can only guess Sire, that he asks for your help against the raiders. It is not my place to ask it, but this is our greatest need. There is nothing else that we require save your good friendship, my lord.' There was a pause.

'Adril,' said the king with a sidelong glance at the girl by his side, 'you shall stay at my court. The days are getting shorter, winter is soon upon us. In spring, you will return to your father's house with one hundred of my cavalry. Captain Sorrell will go with you and supervise the construction of a fort. In the meantime, he will try to teach you the rudiments of swordsmanship and courtly behaviour. Report to me when you are ready to depart.'

The abrupt end of the audience caught Adril by surprise. He had a brief second to stand and bow deeply to the king. A sidelong glance at the princess was rewarded by a meeting of their eyes. Perhaps winter in the palace will not be as cold as expected, he thought.

In the throne room, the king sat quietly for a while, the message lay open on his lap, brief words from another father,

'Cousin, this is my son Adril. He is a loving and intelligent son but prideful. Perhaps you can make something of him.'

The king smiled again remembering his own youth.

Last Train

A radio play for three characters. Death, a passenger, and Mrs Bloom.

('All Aboard!')

'It's a bit crowded today, isn't it? We were lucky to get a seat.'

'Yes, yes, they cancelled the 7.15. These old rattlers can't carry the same number.'

'Oh --, Are you all right? You look very red! That pack must be heavy.'

'Yes, I'm fine, thanks, a little out of breath; I had to run up the stairs.'

'I haven't seen you on this train before, have I?'

'No, I usually get the 7.15. What about you, have we met before?'

'No, I think you'd know if we had. I usually leave an impression.'

'Oh, really? Who are you?'

'I'm Death.'

'Death?'

'Yeah, Death. You know The Grim Reaper, Pale Horseman and all that!'

'Rubbish! You're just a long skinny bloke with a briefcase; probably an accountant!'

'No, really. I just dress like this to fit in. I don't want to scare everyone. I'm actually Death.'

'What are you doing on this train? Is someone going to die? This is a horrible joke. You're making me nervous.'

'You shouldn't be afraid of me. I'm part of life. Think where we would be if no one died. Doesn't everyone like a good funeral?'

'Now, I am scared. Why me? I know I'm a bit overweight, and I drink too much but I'm just a middle-aged bloke with a family and a big mortgage. You don't want me!'

'Oh, I meet different people all the time. I like to find work where I can. Old, young, good, bad, it makes no difference to me. There are plenty of people in this carriage.'

'Oh, God! Is the train going to crash? Are you sure you're on the right train?'

'I can't tell you too much. But not so loud. People are looking. Is this your stop?'

'No, I work at Redfern but why are you doing this? It's a horrible joke, isn't it?

'No, I'm afraid not. You seem a bit stressed. Do you work for the railways?'

'No, No! This is terrible. I'm not ready. I won't have it! I'm getting off here!'

'But it's only North Sydney?'

'I don't care! Let me out! Out of my way!'

('Fair go mate!')

'Hey, you! Yes, you with the pale face! What did you say to that man, you scared him half to death?'

'Oh, not quite that far madam, not yet anyway, believe me. I'll catch up with him later, though. You're Beryl Bloom, aren't you?'

'Yes, how did you know? Have we met?'

'We have now, Mrs Bloom.'

Safe Harbour

The sound of the horn was the growl of a dying giant, low and drawn out. Samuel counted, one, two, three blasts; ship going astern, free to depart. He closed his eyes in the darkness and pictured the scene. Bright sun and gaily flying flags, white hull, streamers tugging at the wharf - a cruise ship, at least in his imagination. The tiny labouring tugs black and workman-like, straining on thin hawsers. Inch by inch they nudge the proud vessel into the stream. He opened his eyes. How long had it been? He could divert his thoughts for a while. Perhaps with practice, he'd do better, make his body servant to his mind but not yet ...

Was it time for a meal? Hunger was a constant companion now. He could no longer use it to estimate the time. He waited for the soft strip of light where he estimated the bottom of the door to be. He knew it was a weakness, but he could not resist the wave of emotion that swept over him, that tiny connection to the outside world. The light would be followed by a sharp scraping sound as his plate was pushed under the door. When would it be?

He had never met his captors, but he knew what they looked like, dark-eyed and wearing their beards like uniforms. Not unlike himself probably, his hair, once a strictly military cut, had grown well beyond his collar. In the dark, he stroked his beard; equal to any of theirs he was sure; and a moustache. None of them would have a moustache.

He shifted painfully on the thin strip of carpet, his only bedding. It gave him little protection from the rough concrete floor. Sleep on his side was impossible. He had long become used to the wasting of his body. A plate of rice each day could not sustain the average human for long, he knew. Prolonging his life was not a priority to them. The inadequate meals were merely another indication that his days were numbered.

He had resigned himself to death. Eventually, the meals would stop, and they would drag him, blinking, into the light for the last time. He did not expect the honour of a firing squad. He was only alive now because of his propaganda value. He and a few others perhaps. As far as he could tell he was the only prisoner in this, … what? If he died, he would be replaced by another poor soul, pawns in power games beyond the battlefield. He would only last as long as he was useful. Perhaps a simple slice of the throat would save the cost of bullets. Would they tell him the night before so they could watch his terror…?

He looked again to where he imagined the door to be. Searching for the thin band of light, a reflection from the dim corridor he suspected. Just enough light to show his gaoler where to push his plate. He had to be impressed; there was never any sound apart from his own breathing. He was grateful for the occasional noise from the port that they could not suppress. It gave him strength that surprised him, a link to an earlier time, bright days of his boyhood.

Sam pulled himself up to the balcony and pointed across the harbour.

'What's that one grandad?

'That's a coal carrier, Sam. Probably loaded up in Balls Head Bay and is on its way to the Northern Rivers. She'll be back soon enough.'

'And what's that one?'

'That's a ferry, as you well know, young lad. You're just trying to trip your old granddad up!', he made a face and reached for the boy. Laughing Sam ducked from his grasp and raced down the steps into the garden.

Was it a little lighter where the door met the floor? He could not be sure. Any time now and the plate would appear, and he would eat. Any time now.

The horn sounded again - two long blasts followed by two short. A vessel wanting to overtake on the starboard side in a narrow channel. Perhaps this was a river port? The cruise liner would be picking up speed now. He closed his eyes. Was the sound real or his mind playing tricks? Did it matter?

He sat on the grass beneath The Bridge, a boy again. Kirribilli at his back, warmed by the sun. The ship moved past with the majesty of a great island blocking the bright sky and white sails of the Opera House. His dream hand rose and saluted the passengers lining her decks. Excited, happy faces, arms waving, perhaps at him or perhaps at a relative on the shore. Tourists could go to distant places. Tourists could lie in idleness on foreign beaches or climb foreign mountains and cathedral steps. And he could go with them. Wherever they went, his imagination could also go.

The grass was uncomfortable. He sat up. Had he been lying down? He could not remember. Why was it so difficult? Painfully he folded his legs in ancient imitation of the Lotus. Why was it painful, he wondered? He let his mind settle. His only world was the bright harbour, but he did not really see it. Thoughts rose and drifted away without reflection. A thin bar of light floated across his vision. Time had no meaning. He floated in nothingness, reluctant to return. He struggled and struggling became fully aware.

More sound from the harbour. Short sharp followed by a muffled blast. Yes, he remembered sounds like that, they had nothing to do with his meal.

He looked again to where he thought the door must be. Was that a faint light at last? In pain, he turned and reached, suddenly ravenous. The glow seemed to flicker; this was different. Change was bad. Where was his plate? A scratching, grinding sound and the glow spread as the door was pushed on rusty hinges. A voice gasped and swore at the fetid air. Stunned by human sounds, Samuel waited for the end. Not even a meal then, before he died.

A pale head thrust through, a smiling hairless face and blinding light. A young male voice announced.

'Time to go, Sam.'

Soft hands assisted. It took him a few moments to understand.

Tyrolean Memories

Ann put down her glass and looked around. Pastel murals, discreetly placed porcelain heating stove, and silver tableware, all spoke of quality and affluence. She fingered the fine linen serviette.

'This seems a pretty expensive place. Can we afford it, Theo?'

I finished my slow mastication of the salmon and mushroom entrée before replying.

'It's not often we celebrate fifteen years of marriage, Ann. Tonight we're making memories. Relax and enjoy the experience.'

I raised my glass and we saluted each other with *Winns' 2014, Back of the Pub,* one of my favourite reds, as we smiled fondly into each other's eyes. Ann was right of course, we couldn't really afford to eat here, but the kids wouldn't suffer much if we tightened our belts for a few months. Fortunately, the conversation moved on.

'This place reminds me of that little café in Bolzano. It was so romantic, wasn't it? Spring in the Italian Alps; sipping coffee in the cobbled plaza. Flowers on every windowsill. It was a wonderful honeymoon, Theo. I'll always remember it.' I smiled in agreement, not wanting to destroy her surge of nostalgia.

How could I forget that café? Its faux Tyrolian facade had struggled for authenticity between a MacDonald's on one side and three almost identical cafes on the other. Plastic fir trees and pinecones for the tourists, waiters in *Lederhosen* and felt hats with feathers. I shouldn't be cynical; it was probably my mood at the time. After three hours by train from Venice, our ever polite hotel manager had insisted that I pay our room deposit in cash. I had to walk two blocks to an ATM while Ann waited with our luggage. Memories.

'I can recall how slick the cobblestones were from the drizzle,' I replied, 'and how we couldn't find the Italian word for *umbrella* in our dictionary.'

'*Ombrello*. From the Latin, as we should have guessed,' she replied, smiling at the memory. I couldn't think of anything to smile about.

'Anyway, the next day we took a local bus to Vincentia to look at the view of the lake from the Abbey. Surely you remember, Theo? It was heavenly, like something from a romantic painting.'

'I think we have a photo somewhere,' I said to cover myself. 'Is that the time we were in that little Fiat bus and you got your foot caught in the seat? It took the driver, and most of the passengers, twenty minutes to extract you, as I recall; and you limped for the rest of the day.'

'I don't recollect any limping, but I do remember the nice young driver with his little hat. He had European charm. Something Australian men don't seem to have. He was handsome too.'

Did I detect a cool tone to her voice?

'I don't remember that,' I lied; I've never been impressed by blonde beards and muscles.

I was considering my next conversational step when the waiter appeared at my elbow, carrying four large plates strung along his arm. On my right, a girl in a colourful *Dirndl* also materialised and our entrée plates disappeared as our main course was served. The interruption gave me time to think about our conversation. Had we been on the same holiday, I wondered?

I offered Ann some potatoes *gratin* from the silver bowl but she declined; there was hardly room on her plate. I added a little to my meal together with a couple of young broccoli.

'How's your hamburger?' I finally asked, knowing the answer.

'Too much bread roll. How is your '*Coq-au-vin*'?

'Delicious,' I replied smiling, 'this whole scene reminds me of the meal you ordered in Bolzano.' I laughed at the thought.

'What do you mean?'

'I remember you ordered *Deutsches Beefsteak*,' I said, 'We waited for ages, and then it didn't even have a salad. I'll never forget your face. You took one small forkful and called the waiter. That's when you found it was their version of *Steak Tartare*. They were not amused when you asked them to cook it'. I laughed.

'Well, I just felt like a steak. How was I to know?' Ann laughed, not to be shaken from her mood.

I topped up our glasses and we sat in silence for a moment.

'Funny, the way we have different memories of the same event. You'd think we'd been on different holidays.' I ventured. Ann met my eyes.

'Keep it up, sport, and I might remember why I married you,' she said, smiling sweetly over her glass as she sipped her wine.

Matchsticks

The world was water; water falling in a warm deluge without wind, vertical, unending. Water in great pellets pitting the surface of the broad grey plain that swept past where the river had once wound between willow-lined banks. Somewhere to the west, the sun cowered behind a grey curtain as though too timid to show its pale face to exhausted humanity.

The boy viewed the scene with the calm security of the innocent. In all his eleven years, he could not remember anything like this. It was new and exciting. He did not fear the violent tumult below the house, the constant drumming of rain on the roof or the serious-faced men who drove past from time to time in noisy timber trucks. His mother told him that they were going upstream to launch a surfboat into the river. If they were successful and pulled with all their strength across the flood, they might be able to reach people stranded on a rooftop out of sight on the far side. He nodded and mimicked her concerned frown, but he did not really understand.

On the tenth day, the rain eased. The sky was still the colour of weathered hardwood, but from his hillside veranda, the boy could now see up the hill to where the road abruptly disappeared on its way to ... somewhere. Or down the hill past other timber houses to the bend where it met the river and took a sudden turn along the bank, following the narrow curve. Only a few isolated drops of rain now added to the flood, yet it continued to rise, like a wild thing refusing to die. In the shadowed foothills where the flood was born, the saturated land still nourished its flow.

The boy put down his comic and looked for a moment over the now-familiar scene. He had seen a rabbit on a log the day before, sailing swiftly past, sole captain of its craft, surviving for the moment but doomed to an uncertain future at the river mouth. Today the view was unchanged, only the sound of rain on the roof was missing. The muddy water still flowed deep and smooth. Branches and tree stumps swept past as before.

A sudden movement near the corner of his eye drew his attention down the hill. The rising water had spurned its usual path and taken a new course cutting through the sharp bend. It flowed between houses and crossed the road. Already more than a foot deep and rising quickly, it ignored paltry human structures. A house at the edge of the road quivered as the water, rushing from behind, swept past its post foundations. A few people gathered where the road was crossed, but there was little they could do. Deeper now and broader; several houses in the new stream shook with a violent jerking motion. Nothing in his life had prepared the boy for this. He could only watch in stunned fascination as, at first slowly then with gathering speed, one house moved with graceful poise from its roadside position, borne by the flood to the centre of the road. Here it seemed to hesitate, shivering, like an animal aware of its fate. The shivering became more violent. Roofing sheet and planks fell as leaves shaken from a dead tree. Still, it struggled and held its shape, transparent, a skeleton without clothes. A squealing grinding sound rose clearly to the listeners on the hill. Then, slowly, the sparse remains appeared to melt. First, the floor, then the windows and finally the jagged frames of the roof disappeared into the flood.

The boy was ordered inside as other houses followed their leader, proud homes reduced in seconds to matchsticks scattered and swept away on the flood.

Kempsey floods, 1949

Absent Friends

Graham poured the wine while the rest of us examined our menus. A Shiraz I think, I couldn't get a look at the label but he asked Jack to bring a corkscrew so it must have been a few years old.

'What did you think of the play?' asked Marie, addressing the table. She likes to keep us focused. Uncontrolled, we might fall into irrelevant chatter and drunken ways. Perhaps even enjoyed ourselves.

'What are you having, Harry?' someone asked. I think it was Jenny.

'I'm having the Godfather,' I said. Jenny raised her eyebrows and feigned interest, but she already knew. I always have the Godfather.

Ann looked at me from the corner of the table, her brow furrowed. We may have been man and wife, but we did not share the same tastes.

'Why don't we have a large one? We can get half Godfather and half Jack's Special, that's vegetarian?'

'We're all sharing anyway, aren't we?' asked Ron.

I sighed inwardly and tried to cast my mind in a wider field. I tasted the wine, not bad, I thought, not bad at all.

'To absent friends.' I said on impulse, raising my glass. Caught by surprise, menus were put aside, and glasses found. I paused dramatically for a long moment.

'To absent friends,' came the jumbled reply and six glasses rose. I am sure they all wondered who was missing. We had been regulars at the theatre for years, and apart from the casual visitor, there were only the six of us. Graham guessed my toast was a conversational gambit and played along.

'Who's missing?' interrupted Marie, still waiting for an answer to her first question.

'Frederick Randal.' said Graham. 'Used to be a neighbour of mine. Walked out the front gate one morning, briefcase and all. He was never seen again.'

Questions hung in the air, words considered.

'Christine O'Connor,' said Marie opposite, getting into the mood. 'We were best friends in school. She became a nun, and I haven't seen her since. I hear she's in the Congo.'

Quicker now, the game afoot.

'Andrew Harvey, my first love. Died in a car crash on this day in 1962', mumbled Jenny, her voice quavering as she put down her glass and stared at the table. All eyes turned to her, but she was in a place of her own. Enjoying the bitter pain of brief happiness.

'Wendy,' said Ron, his voice barely audible. Nobody spoke; we all knew who he meant. 'Died as she gasped for breath, last October....' He would have said more but his mouth just worked for a few moments before he was silent.

There was a long pause. Marie drew a long breath from deep within her chest.

'I didn't like the leading man,' announced Jack, 'I've met undertakers with more life.'

'His wife wasn't any better, nobody could be that dumb,' offered Ann her voice rising in indignation. The rest of us all started speaking at once. Jenny rallied with a visible shudder and sipped her wine. Jack arrived to take our orders. A brief interregnum while order prevailed then the hubbub continued.

And that is how we remembered absent friends; careful not to be the first to leave the table.

Last Meal

April chopped the onion with a brisk economic rhythm. Eggs broke, she beat and folded, adding a little milk and salt.

'Yes, my dear, ready soon.'

Tears welled, and she tried to wipe her eye with the back of her hand, forgetting too late the bruised and swollen socket. She winced and returned to the task. A little oil and she poured the egg into the pan.

Yes, officer, we had a problem with rats. She tried a humourless chuckle but her bruised ribs hurt.

'Almost ready, dear,' she called as she reached under the sink for the final ingredient.

Time About

'**The** Lord giveth and the Lord taketh away .....,'
Sanctimonious, thought Alan. Jack Blake would have laughed,
not that he could do that anymore, lying as he was in a
wooden box about to be burnt at 900 degrees Celsius. The
choir began to sing. The sweet soprano of boys not yet
men. Still, Jack had plenty to laugh about; he had outlasted
most of his peers to reach the age of 108. *Most unusual, even
today*, thought Alan ... except for us. His mind shied away
from the subject that dominated his life.

The singing stopped.

'Grandad was a generous and loving man ...,' began a
new voice, 'we all know that he built a mighty business
empire and became a benefactor to many. But his early
days were not easy. He rarely talked about his youth in
Loboto, hustling on the dusty streets and then moving to
London to work in the diamond business ...,'

The speaker was a short, stocky man with thin lips
combined with a stubby nose and small eyes. Whatever
Jack's other qualities, he had a certain intangible charm that
Tony lacked.

Alan's mind drifted off again, lost in reminiscences. No
one in this church knew that he had once worked with Jack
Blake - or would believe it if he told them.

At the door, he squeezed Tony Blake's offered hand.

'I enjoyed your homily. Your grandfather would have
been proud of you. I'm Alan Reynolds, my father was a
friend of your grandfather.

'Alan Reynolds, yes, delighted to meet you at last. My grandfather and your father were unique people. They left us a wonderful heritage.'

If only you knew, thought Alan, smiling,

'They certainly did,' he said, about to move on.

'You didn't know Old Jack, did you?'

'No, I was born in Australia after my father returned there,' Alan lied, 'But Dad told me a lot about him. He impressed my father deeply.'

'Really?'

'Oh yes, particularly how he managed to rise from simple diamond trading to head a multi-million-dollar, business empire in his lifetime. Very impressive. If I knew how to do that, I'd bottle it!' laughed Alan. Blake looked at him sharply,

'How do you think he did it?'

'I've no idea. Perhaps he picked up something in the mines in Loboto. He got a real leg-up somehow after he left the diamond business, perhaps he found some spare diamonds.' He laughed, 'What do you think?'

'Oh, my grandmother's family helped a lot, I'm sure.', frowning.

A woman in a black floral hat thrust a hand between them and took Tony Blake's in hers. Her face was a mask of grief.

'Tony, I'm so sorry about your loss.'

Alan turned towards the car park. He had only been back in London a few days and already his past was catching up. He would need to be watchful but there was no real danger of revealing his true identity, it had been 78 years, after all. The truth was too implausible. After a few weeks, he would become just another distinguished-looking gentleman in his middle years with the Australian accent and slight limp. The lie repeated often enough became a reality. But no cover was perfect. The ghost of his past was there to be uncovered if anyone bothered to look.

As he opened the car door, he realised he was worried about something. Something that he had seen or heard at the funeral service. It tickled the back of his mind like a half-remembered dream. After a brief mental struggle, he dismissed it from his mind, tomorrow he would pick up Barry and they would drive to the Life Foundation meeting. It would be just another pleasant drive in the English countryside.

It had been interesting and exciting, working in the diamond business. He, Jack Blake and half a dozen others on the trading floor revelling in the cut and thrust of international trade. Although already much older he still retained the youthful appearance and exuberance that the group took for granted and was quickly accepted into their circle. His slight limp, truthfully blamed on a skiing accident in the Australian Alps, simply added to his unusual persona. It was the right decision to come to London and lose twenty years on the trip. The work in the diamond trade was a bonus. He relished the romantic adventure of dealing with buyers from around the world, trading diamonds and currencies, talking to mysterious foreigners with intriguing accents from far-flung places: but eventually, the excitement palled. The long hours and disrupted social life, the resentment at the dulling tedium and long hours, all played their part. He had learnt the diamond business from his father but Jack ... well; he was never sure where Jack had learnt so much. He hinted at an active social life and Alan admitted to a touch of envy for Jack's dark good looks and slight accent. Much later, he realised that he never really knew Jack Blake. The only thing they had in common was the few months they had shared at International Diamonds. After they parted, they would meet again from time to time over the next half-century. Their social lives seemed to be somehow interlinked, like binary stars, coupled by gravity to dance together but never getting too close.

It had all changed when a shipment of diamonds valued at £3,000,000 disappeared. Until then, Alan and Jack had enjoyed a wonderful run. Then everything stopped abruptly. Who would trust a business that could be so careless? Everyone on the floor was interviewed endlessly but there was no suspicion that they had been personally involved. No one really knew where the diamonds had gone. Somewhere between the mine and Heathrow airport was all that they seemed sure about, at first. As far as anyone knew, the diamonds had been loaded on the plane in Loboto and disappeared in mid-air. Later, they could not even be sure that they had reached the airport. Every inch of their journey was investigated without success until, eventually, the authorities grew weary. Old wise heads said not to worry, they would turn up. Diamonds are like fingerprints, they said, each one individual. No one could trade them without giving themselves away. We only need to wait, they said. So they waited and as the days turned to months and the months to years, the trail grew colder. The insurance company paid up and the case became an interesting trade anecdote, a thing of mystery that surfaced occasionally on the back pages of the Sunday paper.

Carlo Allegreti had worked all his life for Tony Blake and with Tony's father before that. He had helped to make the family rich and powerful and, in turn, had become wealthy himself. Near the end of his life, he was content. He stepped into the lift and touched the stud for the penthouse level. The lift responded with a familiar tone and accelerated upward. Tony Blake was more difficult to control than his father but there was no reason for concern. Carlo knew all the secrets; he was one of the family. The lift doors opened onto a panelled vestibule, and he walked a few paces to a door and entered without knocking.

'Good morning, Mr Allegreti, Mr Blake is expecting you.'

'Morning Vivian, you well?' he asked as he passed a woman seated at a small desk. She was blonde, a little overweight and business-like.

'Fine thanks. Would you like some coffee?'

'Yes, thanks. And a couple of chocolate biscuits if you could find some.' It was a comfortable ritual they had enacted many times. He enjoyed adding detail to mundane things.

He reached the next door, pushed it open, and entered.

Tony Blake was not a tall man, and he seemed lost behind the large expanse of antique desk that he affected. Carlo had to admit the desk had to be large to balance the scale of the room and the massive window beyond it. He smiled to himself as he closed the door.

'Carlo, he knows, somehow the bastard knows!' Blake was not a man to contain his emotions. His round face was florid, and his eyes bulged. He spat the words as though his rage would somehow cure the problem. Carlo had often heard such outbursts.

'What are you talking about Tony?

'This damn Alan Reynolds. I spoke to him at the funeral yesterday. As casual as you like he talked about old grandfather Jack's life! He knows things; all about the diamonds; all about the theft. I tell you he knows!'

'Don't panic, Tony. He's probably just guessing. It's been almost 80 years. They'll never trace the diamonds. They're long gone, or we would have heard about it. Probably recut years ago.' Tony was not mollified.

'Who is he, anyway? I've never heard of this Alan Reynolds.' Carlo continued.

'He's the son of a friend of the old man in the diamond business. His father moved back to Australia in the 1980s. Alan grew up there and has just arrived in London. I had Vivian look him up. There's not much information but he seems to be a private investor and entrepreneur. He is also on the board of a biomedical research company,' Carlo was not interested in the details.

'OK, OK, his father knew your grandfather, so what? He knows nothing. If he said something, it's just to scare you.'

'But how could he guess, Carlo? His father must have left some records or something. And even if he is guessing, if any hotshot journalist decides to investigate the old man's involvement, who knows what he might uncover? We could be ruined!'

'Tony, for heaven's sake, settle down. We cannot afford to be hasty. So this Alan Reynolds's father worked with old Jack Blake when Jack lifted the diamonds but only a handful of people know the full story, and he's not one of them. And that's how it will stay. Old Jack founded a great business empire with that diamond money but it hasn't exactly been above-board, has it? He had to hide it, so he spent it wisely and bought influence and paid off public officials. Many people don't want to know where the money came from or hear any more about it.'

'Jesus Carlo! You're not telling me anything new. My family are the only link back to those days. There are people who wouldn't want any digging. That link includes you, by the way!'

'If you're suggesting what I think you are, we have to think very carefully. I know that sometimes we have to be ruthless. God, in your father's day ...'

'No buts, Carlo. Find someone we can trust and make it clean and simple. No loose ends. Any link to the past must die with Alan Reynolds!'

The descent of the lift was a metaphor for Carlo's sunken spirits. It all seemed simple enough, they had done worse in the past, and on less evidence but he thought that that phase was behind them. This was a return to a cruder, more violent time, and he had a bad feeling. Tony was becoming hard to control, perhaps I'm getting too old, he reflected.

Alan turned his vehicle down the ramp and drove towards the lifts. The parking area was nearly full as hotel guests returned from their day in the city. Other hopeful drivers circulated with vain expectations of finding a space. His area near the lift was reserved so he could afford to be relaxed. The large, hired Ford and expensive hotel were an extravagance; a welcome-back gift for himself that he passed off as simple indulgence. He would vacate the hotel when he found a suitable apartment. He stepped from the car and found the remote button as he turned towards the lift. The lights flashed, and a sharp click sounded as the car locked. He was not in a hurry. The bland surroundings faded as he focused a part of his mind on his search for a house and reviewed his plans as he walked. The car park was a concrete box made for cars, dull and economical. Just enough lighting to show the exit signs and concrete pillars. Just enough space to open the doors. He dismissed it from his mind. His first task the next morning would be a call to a couple of estate agents. Then he would lunch at the art gallery as he viewed their catalogue offerings. He was considering a particular

Hilliard miniature and pictured it in his head as he walked. A part of his mind registered routine operations of the car park, the vehicle on the ramp, others passing as he walked.

The Hilliard was a masterpiece, a jewel created by a human mind in the 16th century. A brain long dead, its creation remained.

The sound of the van behind him caught him by surprise but the impatience of the driver saved him. A clumsy effort that spun the wheels with a warning screech without launching the vehicle forward as intended. Alan flung himself sideways without thought. The wing mirror of an expensive Mercedes snapped back as his elbow led his body in flight between the rows. Then he huddled in shaken supplication as the charging van finally found traction and accelerated up the ramp. Someone tried to kill me, he thought in amazement! There could be no other explanation. Why? He sat for a moment in dumb shock as other vehicles passed, then rose and stumbled to the lift. He did not know anyone in London. Why would someone want to kill him? He was still pondering the problem as he stepped into the shower and let the soothing hot water play on his dusty and aching body.

A pleasant drive in the English countryside in the spring, like 'Wind in the Willows' thought Alan idly. Just what was needed after the events of the past few days. Alan had enjoyed the trip down from the city. He and his passenger had chatted for more than an hour. Despite a general similarity, Barry Reynolds looked nothing like his brother. The features that gave Alan his handsome aging-sportsman look somehow combined in Barry in a soft and haphazard way. Alan had not mentioned the attempt on his life. As time passed, he began to wonder whether he had actually imagined it. Perhaps it had just been an incompetent driver. Now he slowed before a high brick fence and followed it to a set of massive wrought-iron gates.

He braked the car briefly as the gates swung slowly open, and then accelerated towards the row of trees at the end of the gravel driveway. The familiar house was very old, large and ivy-covered. A wisp of smoke trailed lazily from one of several clay chimney pots projecting from the high roof. Narrow windows looked out on a strip of lawn that separated the stone walls from the circular driveway and surrounding trees. It nestled in the fold of the hill hidden from the road among the green fields and hedges, hiding like a frightened animal, he thought. What a perfect location for a secret society.

'Looks like we're last here,' said Barry, as he noted the vehicles parked under the overhanging branches. Alan counted ten or more cars and limousines and confirmed the assessment.

'Yes, I think you're right. Maybe they're all a little worried.'

'Well, the meeting's not scheduled to start for another hour, and Peter doesn't like us being all in one spot; it is a little conspicuous.'

'Barry, we've been meeting like this for more than a hundred years. We should have learnt to act the part by now. We are a legitimate research foundation; we have every reason to have board meetings.'

'You're right, of course, but how much longer do we need to hide? Surely we are strong enough to protect ourselves by now?'

'It must have something to do with that collar around your neck, Barry. You always did have an unrealistic opinion of your fellow man. You know as well as I do that if anyone found out that you are 200 years old they might want to take you apart to find out how you did it!'

Barry scowled at his brother, but any further discussion was forestalled. The car circled a nondescript fountain and stopped at broad steps leading up to large wooden doors. Dark windows turned blind eyes to the driveway. A burly pair of uniformed men appeared and quickly gathered the luggage without speaking. Alan recognised a distant nephew, no doubt drafted in for the weekend as security and general help. He picked up a small, battered briefcase and followed Barry up the worn granite steps and into the house.

The boardroom had once been the banquet hall of the mansion. The high vaulted ceiling and decorated entablature shouted out the wealth of the original owners. Polished wood and dark paintings of forgotten people separated several tall windows. Rich velvet curtains helped to retain the image of a time long past. Only the furniture was modern. A broad oval oak table trimmed with leather and comfortable but business-like chairs.

Peter Follard entered briskly and seated himself at the head of the table, placing several sheets of papers down as he did so. Heads turned towards him, and he tapped the table as the hum of conversation subsided. Ten faces regarded him with respectful interest. They were a diverse group, six men, and four women. Their appearances varied but he knew that was deceptive. He was the oldest; age still has its privileges, he mused.

'Before we start the formal business, I have some bad news that just came,' Peter announced. 'Sally and Ibrahim Sampoeno have just been killed in Java. We don't have full details yet but it seems that a neighbour attacked them with a machete.'

Startled gasps and expressions of shock erupted. Alan glanced at his brother across the table.

'But Sally wasn't even one of us,' a female voice exploded.

'Sally was Ibrahim's second wife. She was 83 even with the transfusions, she would not have lived much longer than normal. Ibrahim was 160. He was Andrew's half-brother.' Peter continued, 'I've asked some people from Jakarta to get more information, but I don't expect much. Somehow they gave themselves away.' His voice was soft and hollow.

A stunned silence followed.

'We'll have a brief service for them in the morning but now let's move on with the agenda.'

The mundane details of running a multimillion-dollar organisation took most of the morning. Tea was served as Peter declared the meeting closed and the secretary banished the minutes with a stroke of her finger. They all knew that there would be no record of the rest of the meeting.

'Let's start with Research. Garth, anything to report?'

'Yes, it seems the group of genes we identified in our preliminary studies do not explain our condition.' answered a tall, rangy man at the other end of the table.

'At least, not on their own. We're continuing to investigate whether some combination or particular order of genes, has any influence,' he paused, 'There is one other thing. Fred Smith in Toronto has completed a study of our heritage.' Murmurs of concern sounded around the table,

'Isn't that dangerous? He'd need all our family histories and DNA samples for that, wouldn't he,' asked Barry.

'Yes but we have to take some risks to get answers. We already have all the information on file. Besides, I cleared it with security before I gave the go-ahead.' He glanced at Frank Anderson across the table. Peter's brow furrowed as he tapped the table with his pen to suppress the rising background of questions.

'Let's move on: Did Fred discover anything useful from this study?'

'No, nothing we don't already know. It spreads through both male and female lines and is not weakened by intermarriage with ordinary people. We already number in our hundreds of thousands, and if it continues, we will end up with two races of human. The long-lived and the short-lived.'

'We already have that' said Alan curtly, 'It's just a matter of numbers.' There were murmurs of assent.

'Thanks, Garth: Frank, any comments on security?'

'Well, it's a fact that the larger we get, the harder it is to retain secrecy. In fact, I'm surprised we've come this far without serious leaks. Perhaps our ultimate security would be better served if we started to prepare the general public for the truth. To accept that some people could be much longer-lived than others.'

A babble of voices erupted. 'What about the 'Aliens in our midst' panic of a few years ago?' someone blurted.

Peter tapped the table again, 'We have to be open to all ideas,' he said, 'the rest of you can think about it and bring along your opinions to the next meeting. Helen, what about the villages? How are they going?'

A thin-faced woman answered in a nervous voice,

'We.. we have 97 villages in 24 countries populated with 100% of our own people and another 15 with more than 50%. We have adopted an obscure Buddhist sect as the reason for the exclusive lifestyle. But we also advise our people to interact as much as possible with the surrounding population to avoid antagonism. Education is a problem because the kids don't believe that they are any different from anyone else. That's a little easier to handle in a village school….';

She did not finish the sentence. The table rose on one side, smashed Alan in the face and tumbled Barry onto his back. Sound struck like a club. The windows burst in a million fragments of jagged glass and strafed the room. Part of the ancient ceiling, unable to take the shock, fell into the room showering the stunned occupants with centuries of dust - silence; more falling plaster. Slow eddies of scintillating motes spun in the light from the glassless windows. A primal female wail started up and was joined by a cacophony of moans and coughs. Alan tried to focus his eyes but darkness kept intruding from the edges. It was easier to relax and wait for ....

Waking was the worst part, for an instant, he was back in the smashed room. He marvelled at the redness of the blood and the way the electrical wires swung back and forth; back and forth from the ragged edges of the ceiling. He was lying on something soft: a bed - not the boardroom, a bed. Sharp blades of pain answered any movement.

'He's awake,' someone called from far away. A high-pitched alarm sounded and stopped. Several voices spoke together in tones he could not catch through a dull buzzing in his ears. Light came, and he realised that he was in a well-lit room. He started as the concerned face of a young woman blocked his vision. She wore a stethoscope like a necklace.

'Can you understand what I'm saying?'

'What ... where?' it took a long second to recognise his own voice.

'Don't try to speak, just nod your head.' No need to shout, he thought but nodded anyway.

'Your mouth and throat will be dry from the anaesthetic,' she said, 'Don't try to talk. Have some water.' A plastic bottle with a tube replaced the face. He sucked at the cool liquid and managed to swallow some of it. A whirring sound came from somewhere, and he felt a brief spasm of pain as his head lifted. Barry's face appeared creased with concern.

'You don't look too good,' he smiled.

'But what happened …. ', the voice was a thin whisper.

'A rocket – just good luck that our security people surprised them. They managed to get off one hasty shot but it missed the window and hit the stone wall.'

'Who …,'

'We don't know. They cut a hole in our security fence at the back of the estate. Came across the gardens and through the trees. We're investigating.'

'Who … injured?' Alan managed to express at last.

'Gordon's dead. Malcolm bad but stable – looks like he'll lose a leg. The rest like you, broken bones, concussion. Peter's pretty knocked about but he'll be OK with plenty of rest ….' Alan did not hear any more as the room again receded into darkness.

Blake came around the massive desk with remarkable speed, his fists clenching and unclenching as though seeking a victim or lesser animal to rip asunder. Carlo took a few steps backward. The blood left his face as he prepared to flee.

'What do you mean, 'They missed?' He spat the words with a fury Carlo had rarely seen.

'They were supposed to be professionals. And with a rocket no less! Very subtle!

'What can I say, Tony, we can't get our money back but they won't get their bonus! Better to forget about it and cover ourselves from any investigation.'

'Oh, I'll think of something these clowns can do to make it up. Now Bill Towns owes me twenty thousand, and I'll see he pays somehow.' He paced to the other side of the desk and sat down. 'What happened?'

'It seems they were expected,' Carlo lied, 'they only had time for one shot before they had to shoot their way out. Luckily, they got out alive!'

'Luck, be buggered. More interested in saving their necks than doing the job! What about the police and press? What do they know?'

'Nothing. Neighbours reported explosions but the Foundation just said they were holding a BBQ with fireworks. Some big vans were leaving the estate in a hurry, though.'

'This Alan Reynolds is really starting to annoy me, Carlo! It's the second time we've failed, and people are starting to notice. It's not good for our reputation, and it doesn't solve our problem,' said Blake through clenched teeth.

His words hung in the air as Carlo waited for the outburst to subside.

'Curious, isn't it?' Blake continued, calmer now. 'He didn't report the attempt at the house. Even the hit-and-run was just reported as a road incident. And that by a witness. It's now 24 hours, and there are no news reports of a rocket attack, for Christ's sake! I was wondering whether he was hiding something but now a whole organisation. What are they up to?' He returned to his desk and sat down.

Carlo tried to look thoughtful and did not interrupt.

'Get out of here and get me my $20,000 back and send Vivian in as you go. I want to find out about this Foundation.'

Blake drew himself from the pool and reached for the offered towel. If he was at all embarrassed about his pallid skin and generous paunch, he didn't show it. Carlo wiped the sweat from his forehead and loosened his tie. Carlo didn't share Tony Blake's liking for saunas and heated swimming pools. Frowning, he returned to the table against the wall and reached for his glass of orange juice. Tony joined him and slumped into a plastic chair.

'OK, Carlo, let's review; Life Foundation is a private bioresearch foundation with offices in almost every county.'

'A great cover if you needed one' interjected Carlo, Blake ignored him.

'Their main research divisions are in Australia, the US and Britain but they have laboratories in many other places. Their main research area is the genetics of aging, although they have many other projects running concurrently. Anything else?'

'Maybe. Does it strike you that this Foundation is a little strange?' asked Carlo.

'In what way?' Blake wanted to move on but he valued Carlo's opinion.

'They are very low-profile. Bland name; no major office buildings; a foundation not listed on the stock exchange. They are a multi-national leader in genetics apparently but no one outside their field has heard much about them. I've searched the press: it's almost as though they are invisible. Very few stories of breakthroughs or research expectations, even in the science press. No promotions for funds. They don't even have a PR department. But how does any of this help us get rid of Reynolds?'

'Yeh, I know what you mean, Carlo, something is going on here. They're hiding something valuable. I'd like to know what it is as well as get rid of Reynolds. But you're right, let's not get ahead of ourselves. Alan Reynolds is a member of Life Foundation, but he also knows about old Jack and the diamonds. We'll have to finish the job with him while we're getting reports on the board members. If they're up to something, this could be a new direction for us.'

'Yeah, you're right, Tony,' mumbled Carlo without conviction.

'Get back to your office. I want that information tomorrow. Be in my office at 9.30 and bring everything with you.'

'Yeah, sure, Tony,' mumbled Carlo as he turned towards the door.

The view from the 21st floor was sombre. Dark clouds rolled from the south and flashes on the horizon heralded the approach of a dramatic change. Blake turned away from the scene.

'Carlo, this report on the Life Foundation. There's something not right,' Tony's voice rose in a question mark.

'What do you mean?' answered Carlo flatly, not knowing what to expect.

'The board members, Peter Folliard, Alan Reynolds and the others, their biographies are immaculate. But there is something I can't put my finger on.' He flicked the pages in exasperation. Four biographies, each two pages long, thumbnail picture on the left ....

'Did your man use a template to write these up, Carlo? They're so uniform, at least until recently. Each one has a kindergarten report, secondary school report, university admission, job references. The text changes, the names are different but it's as though they came from the same factory. What's going on?

'I'll have a word with the agency. It's probably just the way they collect the info.'

'Yeah, maybe. But it's extraordinary. All the details are from the last twenty years or so. Get me some interviews with their teachers and school friends.'

'Yeah, sure, Tony.'

'And while you're at it, expand your search to include similar names. If these documents are false, they probably stole some dead person's identity or something like that.'

Outside a flash of lightning, much closer now, revealed for a moment the river and sleeping city.

The mall was thinly crowded when the third attack came. A group of three rapid shots shattered the glass in a shopfront and terminated an unlucky near-naked mannequin sunning herself in a travel agents window. Alan might have been similarly dispatched had his phone not sounded, stopping him in mid-stride. As the glass fell about him, he had no time to ponder who might have been trying to call him or to reach the phone in his pocket. For a brief second, he cowered half bent. If the killer had waited a second before fleeing, he might have been more successful. Witnesses would later report one man carrying a toolbox, just a man wearing a cap of some kind, on the atrium's second level.

'Just pulled out a gun, with a long barrel thing, 'fhit, fhit, fhit' not very loud! Sorry officer, I was too busy looking at the gun!'

Alan knew none of this. As shocked shoppers stood about in stunned silence, he continued feigning calm and left the building through the next exit. There was no doubt now that someone was trying to kill him. Was it because he was a long life? Who would know? He would have to tell the Foundation. Peter Folliard or Frank Anderson were the only ones he could talk it over with.

'I don't know Alan; those were attempted assassinations. If it were just about Long-Life it would either be a spontaneous expression of envy and xenophobia or an enquiry about how we do it. This was planned, measured. This person simply wants you dead. Whoever is doing this either hates you for a personal reason, or he wants you dead because you know something about him that he wants to keep secret. You need to think about it.' Frank spoke with passion and frustration. It was clear that the problem that Alan had brought him was a potential disaster.

Alan regarded him across the small table of the cafe. The early summer sun warmed his back, and the sounds of the rowers calling the strokes rose faintly from the river below.

'But I've tried, Frank. I can't think of anything. As far as I know, I have not offended anyone, I have no enemies. I've only been back in London a few weeks. I've avoided the place for 78 years, for heaven's sake! All the short lifers from the old days are gone. I went to the funeral of the last one a week ago ....' His voice trailed off.

Anderson lowered his coffee cup.

'What is it?'

'Jack Blake. I was at his funeral last week. The first attack was a few days later.'

'Did you speak to anyone?'

'Yes, his grandson, Tony Blake, but I didn't tell him anything.' He finished hurriedly. 'He thinks it was my father who knew Jack. Everything is in place.'

'Think about what you said. Did you discuss your 'father's' life with this Jack?' Frank raised both hands signalling the appropriate punctuation.

'Well, yes but nothing he could connect to us.'

'Then it must be something you said, some detail. They're a pretty mysterious bunch, the Blakes. Very powerful. And there are plenty of rumour, connections to the mobs, etcetera.'

'I'm trying to think. We were talking about 'father's' time in the diamond trade with old Jack ....' In his mind, he connected again with the Jack he knew when they were young. What had he said? What secret had he revealed? He thought he had been careful, long-lifers are trained not to reveal, by inference or detail, that they have walked in their fathers' shoes. What could he have said? Did he give his long life away, or was it something else?

'There was that business with the stolen diamonds but all of us, including Jack, were cleared of any involvement. I only mentioned it as an interesting thing that I had heard about. I didn't accuse Jack of anything. It was 81 years ago!'

'Could Jack actually have been involved?' asked Frank Anderson.

'Well, he would have known how to do it. He grew up in Loboto, and he knew all the people and all the systems.'

'That has to be it, Blake thinks that you know how his grandfather stole the diamonds and doesn't want you telling. Even if you don't know yourself, he doesn't want you following the trail of breadcrumbs and unravelling the truth if you write a book or something.' He stood up suddenly,

'This place is secure; it belongs to one of our people but I can't guarantee anywhere else. You are probably being followed. Leave your car here for the moment. Someone will pick it up. I'll drop you somewhere public and secure.'

Alan did not speak as they left the little café and crossed the few paces to Frank's car.

Alan scribbled final notes and threw down his pen. The screen cast a pale glow over the desk and the walls of the booth. Early gloom had captured the streets as the city outside settled down for the night and the evening crowd of browsers and students had not yet invaded the library. He pushed back his chair and leant back. It's not hard to join the dots when you know where the dots lead; a little like

48

following a trail of breadcrumbs as Frank had said. Alan's memory had been ignited by his chat with Frank Anderson and the brief meeting with Tony Blake at the funeral. Perhaps the sounds and smells of London after all this time had helped to revive his mind. All he needed was to check the dates and one or two facts to confirm something that had been at the back of his brain for three-quarters of a century. There was no proof but he was as certain of it as he was of his own existence; Jack Blake had stolen those diamonds and arranged the murders of the couriers, most likely. He sent the files to the garbage bin and cleared the screen. No one would ask about his interest in a long-dead case. Picking up his briefcase, he hurried from the building and was soon lost in the throng of commuters now crowding the streets.

He had made a discovery, scratched an irritation on his mind but what would he do now? Write a book? He did not consider going to the police, it was better for all his kind if he kept quiet and avoided attention. He could never be certain that his cover would survive a really rigorous investigation. He needed to talk it over with Frank again. Feeling more relaxed now, he hailed a cruising taxi and gave the driver directions.

Tony Blake was not a happy man. In a few short days, Alan Reynolds had managed to disrupt his life completely. He should have been quickly eliminated so that Blake could turn back to his other enterprises but the man persisted in thwarting his plans.

Vivian entered and strode across the expanse of carpet to his desk. Blake looked up and regarded her critically. The faint wisp of perfume distracted him for a moment but he raised his eyebrows in question.

'I have those reports on the Life Foundation, Mr Blake. Do you want them now?'

'Of course I do, Vivian! It's been a week. What took so long?'

'I kept asking, Mr Blake. They told me some of the information was very difficult to get. Big gaps in the records or something. I'll bring them in.'

Twenty minutes later, he put down the first set of reports. He had never seen records like these. The three men did not appear to have been born despite the authentic-looking certificates. None of their teachers or childhood friends could be found. There were no school records when there should have been. Their histories before the age of about 45 were clearly fake. With a resigned sigh, he picked up a thick parcel of similar names and began reading.

Alan's father Harold had arrived in London from Australia in 1959 aged 25. He returned to Sydney in 1982 age 48. Records show that he entered the country on 2nd June 1982 then, nothing more. Shortly after that the name Alan Reynolds appears. All but three of the 'Alan Reynolds' have clear records from birth. None seem to have any connection with London. Of the remaining three, one was in prison, and the other was currently a parliament member. The third, marked for further investigation, was sketchy. Alan Reynolds, born 1985 in Sydney, attends Crow's Nest Technological College, (no record), leaves school in 2002 and opens a diamond trading business! He must be in business with his father but there is no record of it. Why put everything in his son's name? The documents also show that he bought a house in 2004 aged 19. *'This character must be some sort of child prodigy.'* Thought Tony. Anyway, it could not be his Alan Reynolds, that person would now be aged 75 but the person he knew was barely more than middle-aged. It was all too confusing. None of the birth dates were absolutely certain. He drew a line through the items that the investigators could not absolutely confirm. One line stood out; Alan's birthday. It looked genuine but could he be sure? Did it matter? If it was not authentic, what were the implications? Either Alan had changed his birth date for some reason, or he was not Alan Reynolds.

He looked at the columns again. There was another possibility; old Harold's details were confirmed from multiple sources up to his age of 68 in 2002, and then stopped. Alan's confirmed details began in the same year and continued to the present. Easily explained if Harry and Alan were the same person. But of course, that was impossible otherwise he would be 146, clearly impossible. Blake threw down his pen in frustration. He had been puzzling over the problem for an hour and, apart from confirming that Alan Reynolds was hiding something, he was no nearer the truth.

Carlo entered to find Blake standing by the tall window looking out on the city. The Thames wound its way far below, and darkness was yet to settle on the spires and deep shadows of Westminster.

'Find anything?' he asked.

'Yes and no. He's hiding something, our Alan Reynolds, him and his father. But I can't put my finger on what it is. He is certainly not the man he claims to be, and neither was his father.' He turned to the older man decisively.

'Here, take the files for Peter Follard and Garth Andrews and see if you can find something. Look at their fathers' lives too.'

'OK, I'll do it when I get back to my office. I wanted ......'

'Do it now, here. I'll wait, I've got other work to get on with but I want to get to the bottom of this.' Blake snarled.

Carlo snatched up the files and marched out of the room, this was not the time to challenge Tony Blake. Had there ever been?

Alan considered the small masterpiece in front of him; a Jean Clouet miniature that the gallery displayed to a limited number of possible buyers. But he could not concentrate. The events of the past few days consumed his mind and excluded all other thoughts. His mood of anticipation and excitement at returning to London was now shattered, replaced with a dark feeling of impending disaster. Someone wanted him dead. They could strike at any time. He was confident he knew who they were but could not report them to the authorities without risking an investigation and awkward questions about himself and the Foundation. There was nothing he could do.

He stood back from the Clouet with a sigh and turned to the tall, formally dressed man beside him.

'I'm sorry, Mr Farac, I can't concentrate today. I'll have to think it over.'

'Certainly, Mr Reynolds. Just call me anytime you want to look.'

Alan thanked him again and made a short call on his phone. He then left the building through a side entrance. A white sedan driven by a large man pulled up immediately in front, and he stepped into the back seat. The driver had a round face framed by abundant curly brown hair. A black chauffer's cap sat awkwardly on his head and a thin cable, coiled like a pig's tail, draped from his right ear and disappeared into his spotless black jacket.

'Thanks, George.'

'My pleasure, Mr Reynolds. Where too?'

'Just drive for a while George, I want to think.'

George was on loan from the Foundation and Alan had soon developed a liking for his quiet confidence and professional manner. It was reassuring to know that Frank Anderson was already gathering security information that might assist them. Alan was acutely aware that this situation threatened them all. Blake may have thought that his mob connections would allow him to easily eliminate an irritation. He was yet to learn what the Foundation and its billion-dollar resources, could do.

The large white Ford had been weaving aimlessly through south London's streets for ten minutes when Alan pulled his phone from his pocket and made a call. He spoke as soon as a voice answered,

'I have an idea. Can we meet?'

After listening for a few minutes, he cancelled the call and put the phone away.

'Hyde Park, George.'

'Yes, Mr Reynolds.'

It was a formality; Alan knew that George had already received detailed orders where to meet. It was a comfort, though slight, to know that others were also interested in his welfare. He settled back into the plush seat and tried to turn his thoughts to other matters.

Alan's meeting with Frank Anderson was short but secure. Their only protection was their isolation but that also made it a perfect place for an attack. Fortunately, two vehicles parked under an oak tree on a minor access road did not draw attention. They saw no one; few people came here except for the occasional jogger.

The two men walked together a short distance up a narrow path that bordered the road. Alan did most of the talking at the start. Frank's face reflected his scepticism as

Alan began but as he continued to talk his posture took on an attitude of interest. He spoke only briefly until Alan had finished, then,

'It's complicated Alan, and it will need to be carefully thought through and executed but it might just work. At least it could help us control the situation. Anyway, it's the only plan that we have at the moment. I'll have my office check a few details and begin the process. We will need to be very secure. Blake is not a fool, and he has a lot of resources.' He stopped and faced Alan on the path his face creased with concern. 'One other thing, Alan. You know where this is going. If we are successful people will probably die. Can you live with that?'

'If we don't do it, I will be killed no matter how much you try to protect me. But apart from that, our secret will be out, and many more could die. I don't like it but it has to be done, Frank.'

'OK, Well done! You'll be doing my job soon!' Frank finished the conversation with a smile.

If Tony Blake wanted to kill Alan Reynolds, he would not find it an easy job now but the real problem was much greater. Blake had to be completely neutralised, and anything he knew about the Foundation expunged. In short, he had to go and his knowledge and suspicions with him.

A week later, a small man wearing a trilby and a dark gabardine coat disembarked at Holborn Tube station and walked along Kingsway. In one hand he carried a large briefcase and in the other a furled black umbrella. The sky was overcast, and a few drops of rain had already begun but he did not stop to unfurl his umbrella. He turned into Twyford Place and searched the polished brass plaques for a name and street number. Finding one to his satisfaction, he ascended the few steps into the building.

Carlo Allegreti's office was on the ground floor. Nothing ornate, merely a pair of glass doors with the name, Allegreti Solicitors etched in large letters. The small man entered and approached the reception desk.

The girl polishing her nails was caught by surprise. Clients visiting at any time were unusual and a morning visit particularly so. She opened her mouth but before she could speak, the man said.

'I have a package for Carlo Allegreti, can I leave it here?'

'Err, yes, of course. Who shall I say it's from?'

'All the information needed is in the packet, I understand. I'm just the poor courier.' He laughed and placed a large package on the counter.

'I'll leave it with you then. Cheerio,' he turned and was already out the door before the girl, open-mouthed, reached for the phone.

It was a large white padded postal bag printed in black with touches of red - a standard Post Office bag like those produced by their thousands. Extra-wide brown tape sealed it from end to end. Carlo considered the packet carefully. He had survived in a hostile world due to his natural caution, and he liked it that way. Judging by its size and weight the package contained a sizable sheaf of papers but how to be sure? He came to a sudden decision, inserted a bronze letter opener, and quickly split the seal at one end. He looked inside cautiously before reaching in and drawing out the contents. A thick file of standard size typed sheets neatly bound along one edge and another thick envelope on top. He knew what was in the envelope before he opened it. The size and shape were very familiar to him, but he sat in stunned disbelief at the sight of £1,000,000 in large denominations arranged in a slab of neat bundles with the bank's wrapping band still attached. He searched in vain for any message.

Carlo's mood of stunned disbelief was abruptly disrupted by the telephone.

'What is it, Sashi?' He had too much on his mind to worry about minor office matters.

'A man on the phone, Mr Allegreti. He won't give his name; he's very insistent. He wants to talk to you,'

'Oh, all right, put him on.'

'Here he is now, Mr. Allegreti.'

'Hello, who is this, and what can I do for you?' Carlo could not afford to offend people who would not leave their names.

'The package on your desk contains £1,000,000 and a substantial file of papers, Mr Allegreti. I think that should be introduction enough.' There was a long pause.

'Are you still there, Mr. Allegreti?'

'Yes, of course, what do you want?'

'We want you to give the file to your associate, Mr Blake. The money you can keep. It is simply a tool to establish our bona fides. There is no need for anyone else to know about it. I will call you again in a few days. Just remember the name, Blackbird. It is not my real name, by the way.' The line went dead before Carlo could answer.

Carlo slumped back in his chair. Minutes later, he broke from his thoughts and pressed a button.

'Sashi, bring me a coffee. Make it strong.'

He knew he was being compromised. He had done it often enough to others. But what did 'Blackbird' want? Whatever it was it must be vital to him, £1 million was a lot of money. He reached for the file and began reading. An hour later he closed the last page and pushed it away. This was nothing less than a complete history of the Blake family for the past three generations. At least a record of their criminal activities. It included information that Carlo did not himself suspect and other matters thought long forgotten, like the diamond theft in 1961. He came to a decision.

'Sashi, go get yourself a coffee, tea or buy a dress or something, for an hour. I'll mind the shop.'

Sashi gathered her coat and purse and left the office. She had learnt not to question her boss's occasional eccentricities. She was puzzled when she returned to find a light burning in the alcove that the copy machine shared with the tea-making facilities. She was not surprised to find that the device was almost empty of paper. Carlo would present the file to Tony; it would be interesting to watch his face but a little insurance was always a good idea. There was no need for him to know about the money.

The early morning was Carlo's special time. He had enjoyed breakfast with his family, and after the loss of his wife, his grandchildren. Now it was just a housekeeper and the morning paper; still, he cherished the time and was not pleased when the telephone sounded as he buttered his last piece of toast.

'Good morning Mr Allegreti. How are you this morning?'

'You again, what do you want? How did you get this number?'

'Let's not waste time on details. We noticed that the £1 million we gave you has been deposited in your Isle of Wight account. Mr Allegreti. Very wise, there is no need for the British tax regulators to become involved, is there?'

'I asked you what you wanted!' there was no point in asking how they knew about his retirement fund.

'We would like to add a little to your nest egg Mr Allegreti. Not quite as much this time, just £500,000. We want you to do us a small favour.'

'Now why would I do you any favours for any amount of money? You can go to hell.' He barked the words with frustration.

'Having taken our £1 million, you could say it would be the honourable thing to do us a small service. There is also another minor point. Mr Blake might not be impressed by his trusted associate taking money from another organisation. It's up to you, Mr Allegreti.'

'What is this 'service' that you want from me?' He needed time to think.

'You have arranged three attempts on the life of someone who we are very interested in; please don't bother to deny it; we want to know when and where the next attempt will take place.'

'Why, so you can protect your pretty boy Alan Reynolds?'

'On the contrary, we could give your assassin every assistance. But enough talk. I'll call you again in four hours.' The line went dead.

What harm could it do? At the very worst, Blackbird and whoever he represented would interfere, and Reynolds would live. That was no skin off Carlo's nose. Blake could always try again; on the other hand, if they helped somehow, as Blackbird suggested, it could be the difference between success and failure. And it would be best if Blake did not know about any of this. He thought for a few minutes then picked up the phone and punched a number.

When the now-familiar voice called again he did not waste time, 'Reynolds's car, tomorrow morning. Half a kilo of Semtex under the seat. When do I get the money?'

Alan's hand trembled as he picked up the phone and spoke the name.

'Tony Blake'

The screen flashed and a female voice answered with a question.

'Calling Tony Blake?'

He confirmed and heard the familiar tones, then;

'Hello, Tony Blake', his voice was sharp and crisp.

'Hello Tony, this is Alan Reynolds,' there was a long pause.

'Alan, I must say you surprise me. What can I do for you?' He seemed genuinely surprised.

'Let's not pretend Tony. You're trying to kill me. I'd like to know what I need to do for you to call your killers off. Did you get the file?' He was calmer now that the plan was underway.

'I thought that stack of paper must be from you, Alan. What is it, counter insurance of some kind?'

'I'm glad you appreciate the situation, Tony. At the moment I am the only one who has put it all together, but the files speak for themselves, don't they? I'm sure that one of your excellent London papers would be very interested in the story. Don't you think?' He tried to sound confident but firing all your guns in one salvo was a desperate move.

'Surely you not suggesting a trade-off, are you?' said Blake.

'Why not?'

'Well for one thing, there is the small matter of your Life Foundation. If you know all about me and my family, I'm sure that they do too, after all 150 years is a long memory, don't you think, Alan?' There was another long pause. Alan decided to play ignorant despite his flush of disappointment.

'What are you talking about?'

'I couldn't figure it out at first,' said Blake. 'All those false histories and birth certificates. So I decided to start close to home. Old granddad was a bit of a lad before he settled down. He often appeared in the social pages, someone even snapped him at International Diamonds Inc. It looks like a group at a Christmas party, 1962 I think, and guess what, you're also in the picture!' so the truth was out, thought Alan. It remained to be seen what Blake would do with it.

'Rubbish Tony, 98 years ago, you know that's impossible!'

'You're ahead of me, Alan. Yesterday I would have thought so too but now it all fits.' Blake answered. Alan paused before replying. Did he sound vulnerable enough?

'You seem to know a great deal Tony but clearly these are things better not discussed over the phone. Can we meet somewhere?'

'Sure, what do you have in mind?' replied Blake brightly. He is obviously enjoying this, thought Alan.

'Forgive me if I'm a little cautious but I think we need some common ground. What about Wellfield Common, midnight tonight. Come unarmed and bring Carlo Allegreti with you but no one else. Just you and Carlo, we'll provide the transport.' He did not need to pretend to be nervous.

'A little melodramatic but OK. Why Carlo? And what's this about the transport?'

'You've tried to kill me three times and I've read the files. Carlo's your right-hand man. I want him in front of me not behind. As for the transport, I want us on equal terms. We'll be watching, try any trick and we'll see them.'

'OK, OK agreed, send the car, out front at 11.10pm,' said Blake. He was not concerned with details.

'Good', said Allan and hung up.

Blake looked at his watch and stood up,

'Time to go, Carlo,' he said as he led the way to the lift. Carlo followed.

'I don't like it, Tony,' said Carlo as they waited. 'You don't expect him to just hand over the biggest secret in history, do you? And what about the files? He still knows about the diamonds. He can double-cross us at any time.'

'Mr. Reynolds will not live long enough to double-cross anyone. Arrangements have been made. He'll be dead before morning tea tomorrow.'

'You've got another hit planned!' Carlo tried to sound surprised.

'He'll try to persuade me about mutual destruction. He won't reveal my secret if I don't reveal his. But if he's dead, I can squash any enquiries the release of the files can cause. The main problem is to get rid of him.'

They walked out the front door into a light drizzle. Light from the building foyer and streetlights cast confused shadows on the dim street. A large man dressed as a chauffeur hurried from the protection of the building portico and approached them.

'Mr. Allegreti? This is your car, sir. Just call us when you want it picked up.' He said as he indicated a white sedan immediately in front.

'Here are the keys.' Carlo took the offered key and the large man turned and walked away without a word, unfurling an umbrella as he did so.

'Search the car, Carlo. I don't want any tricks either.'

Carlo unlocked the passenger door and looked inside. The car looked and smelt like a hire car should. The little triangular cardboard sign swung gently from the rear vision mirror and fresh paper mats covered the drivers and passenger floors. Carlo moved to the driver's side, half closing the door against the drifting rain. The hire papers were in the glove box. The car was fully insured and hired for unlimited mileage for seven days. The hirer, Mr Smith, had even ticked the box allowing a second driver. How considerate, thought Carlo without humour. Ten minutes later, he slammed the boot and stood back. A thorough search had revealed nothing. Tony stood at a safe distance while Carlo started the car. Finally satisfied, they started off on the twenty-minute trip to Wellfield Common.

There was little traffic and they made good time on the M4 before the Braxton turnoff. The car was alone on the road when it reached the roundabout at Willoughby. It was halfway around the right-hand turn when the explosion tore it into a misshapen mess of metal and burning plastic. Flying lumps of debris fell to the wet road casting fluttering shadows for several minutes before the flames finally succumbed to the rain and darkness reclaimed the intersection.

Frank Anderson put his phone away and turned to Alan his face a picture of satisfaction.

'It's done, confirmed, they're both dead, killed by the bomb meant for you.' He said briskly. Alan felt a little sick in the stomach.

'Don't feel bad about it. It was on a timer; all George did was make sure that it didn't go off before delivering the car. Just remember it was meant for you.' They were silent for several minutes before Alan spoke, his voice soft and distant.

'It's just the start, you know. Maybe Garth was right, we have to start educating the public to accept us in some way.' Frank nodded without speaking. They shook hands and Alan picked up his briefcase with the precious Clouet and walked into the night.

Salvation

We came ashore on February 12, 1846: it was a Tuesday. There were three of us now, Johnson, Ellis and me. Reynolds had died as we crossed the reef, a bitter irony. He was already delirious when we first sighted land and I doubt he heard our cheers as the stern of the longboat lifted on the light swell and we pulled towards the beach.

In the quieter waters of the lagoon, we regarded the scene before us. The thick jungle in the hinterland thinned to a light scatter of palms and ferns nearer to the shore but there was no sign of life; no inkling of civilisation. We did not talk, each of us understanding in his own way. We had survived mutiny and fire but providence had set a new test before us.

I nodded my agreement to Ellis and he guided our craft towards a low peak of rock at the end of the beach. With failing strength, we found a quiet lee and ran the boat onto the sand. Johnson was fully spent but Ellis managed to stumble over the gunwale onto the sand. He knelt for a moment in silent supplication then received a line from me with which he quickly secured the vessel against the gentle surge of the sea. I too gave thanks for our safe harbour then looked to Johnson who slumped across his oar. Our arrival in our new home was complete.

After a few moments rest, Johnson appeared to revive a little and with threats and encouragement Ellis and I managed to get him onto the beach. The three of us stood on Terra Firma at last. Only now would I allow myself the release of remorse and my tears flowed unabated. Only three souls alive of 132 entrusted to my care. A just god should strike me down for such a crime!

Though we could barely move from exhaustion I used my tongue to effect and drove the others to unload the boat. Night was approaching and we had neither water nor protection. We walked a little inland among the brushes and palms near the shore and piled our provisions in a small clearing. I set Johnson the task of finding firewood while I fetched more stores from the boat. Ellis, I judged to be better equipped by intellect and nature, and I set him the task of finding a supply of fresh water before the light faded. His dark face seemed almost grey with exposure and fatigue but he did not object. I handed him the musket and bade him not to waste ball and powder if it could be avoided. If anyone could secure our survival it would be him but how much of the teachings of his mother's people he had retained I could not judge.

I had barely returned from the beach when Johnson appeared from among the ferns clutching a few twigs and bark. With harsh words, I sent him to scan the shoreline for driftwood while I unpacked flint and steel. Soon we had a small fire going and I spread some fern fronds to make smoke. Perhaps it would guide or encourage Ellis, there was little more we could do but await his return so we sat in weary silence as the sun exhausted its final spark and sank below the waves. Almost immediately we started to the sound of feet on sand. Ellis appeared in the dim glow from the fire. Without a word he handed me the small flask that he had carried for water and I perceived by its weight that he had been successful. I uncapped it and tasted. Oh, what sweet elixir! No wine could taste so pure and good. I handed it to Johnson across the fire and he too drank deeply. So occupied were we with the water that it was not until we had slaked our thirst that we noticed that Ellis carried something else. I insisted that he bring it forth. Without preparation or preamble, a large lizard was thrown onto the fire scattering twigs and coals in all directions. Johnson took a rapid step backwards in shock but I perceived the creature to be dead and no longer a threat. In his usual snivelling tones Johnson demanded to know what we were expected to do with it. Ellis replied reasonably that we could eat or starve; it was all the same to him.

I will not bore you with details of the time we spent on Tuesday Island. We quickly fell into the roles best suited to our survival. Ellis was dominant as the hunter; I fetched water and found new pleasure in teaching my hands to make useful utensils and hunting tools for Ellis. Johnson did not appear to have any useful skills but would carry out simple tasks willingly enough when directed. So, the days turned to weeks and the weeks accrued. Ellis found new sources of food. A fat sea bird that made burrows in the tussock grass on the headland was easily caught but not at all palatable, being stringy and greasy. Of lizards there was a constant supply but in spite of filling our bellies we never learnt to enjoy them. In his constant search for variety Ellis bade me make him a long spear with three prongs on the end that he would use for fishing. I suspected that he knew quite well how such a spear could be fashioned but he insisted that I do it. Johnson also deferred to him and I did not object. In other circumstances he could have been our leader.

Each day we gathered firewood and piled it ready in the event that we should see a ship. Each day we took turns to climb the rock and look out to sea. Wood became scarce and we were forced to search further and further from our camp. The palm hearts that we so relished as a salad became difficult to find. Would fish and fowl follow?

I was removing the feathers from one of the fat birds when Johnson's excited shout issued from the end of the beach. I saw his arms waving as he gesticulated wildly to the west but I could not perceive any sign of a ship on the horizon. Still, I wasted no time in throwing a great load of wood on the fire and stoking it furiously, by the time it was ablaze, Johnson had reached the camp and declared that he had seen a ship from his position on the crag. Ellis, who had arrived from the forest as silently as ever, helped us as we rudely ripped green ferns and threw them onto the fire. Soon a great cloud of white smoke ascended in the light breeze.

I swear none of us breathed as we waited and watched. Johnson wanted to go back to his perch on the rock but Ellis forbade him. It would serve no purpose. Many minutes followed without any sign or human movement. I began to think that Johnson's fantasy had got the better of him. A low bank of cloud on the horizon perhaps? Then Ellis, keener eyed that we, shouted, 'A sail! A sail! I see it by God a sail!' and dropped to his knees. A few minutes more and we could all see it. A small schooner approaching the island making slow progress close hauled on a starboard tack. Finally, she stood off our beach and launched her jolly boat. Oh, the joy in our hearts as the hope of our rescue was finally realised. We ran forward to meet her, and then stopped for a moment as though afraid the scene was a fantasy that would vanish before our eyes. Ellis and I exchanged glances. Johnson and the rowers shouted as the boat grounded on the beach.

Then I stepped forward and shook the boatswain's hand. It was March the 12th 1846.

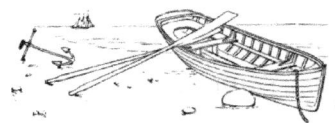

Ham Radio

'**G**ood morning listeners! This is Rodney Reynard and today I'm talking to Mrs Alice Wolf, recently widowed in the Pigtown incident!'

'Good morning, Mrs Wolf!'

'Good morning, Rodney.'

'Now Mrs Wolf, in a moment I'm going to ask you a few questions about Mr Wolf and the tragedy but first please tell our listeners a few things about yourself.'

'Yeh, sure Rodney, there is not much to tell but what would you like to know?'

'You've been married about three years and you have three young pups, is that correct?'

'Yes, that's right. The first is Nigel and then there's Wendy and then it's Horrible, Rodney.'

'What was that?'

'Not you Rodney! No, that's his name, Horrible. He's so much like his father, so we called him Horrible.'

'That's nice, Alice. What about you? Tell our listeners about yourself.'

'Not much to tell, Rodney. I was married straight out of the den and I've been a mother ever since. I tried to help BB but he was the breadwinner. He ... He... (sob).'

'It's all right, Alice. I'm sure that our listeners understand. It's a very emotional time for you. Let's talk about BB if you can. How did he get the name BB?'

'Thanks, Rodney. I'll be OK. Yes, BB, his parents tried to give him a good start in life, so they called him Big Bad to make him sound scary. Then his school friends shortened it to BB. He was big and wonderful and brave. He … (sob).'

'Alice, I have to ask you; what was he doing in Pig-town that night?'

'Well, Rodney, he is …, was … a family man, you know. He had to bring home the bacon. It should have been easy, straw house and all.'

'A warning to us all perhaps, Alice. Did he get careless, do you think?'

'Yes, that's all I can think of Rodney. Perhaps the smell of all that ham was too much for him.'

'There are eye-witness reports that he had already destroyed two houses, one of straw and one of sticks, before he got to the last one. That's amazing, Alice! How could he have done that?'

'Oh, he was a very powerful wolf, Rodney. He would just huff and puff. Not much could stand in his way.'

'I don't want to upset you, Alice but our listeners will want to know; the pigs, the pot, the fire – they were all found at a brick house. Do you think that had anything to do with it?'

'No doubt about it, Rodney! (Water? Yes, thank you.) Yes, the brick house. It's the classic wolf trap, Rodney. Easy straw house, then a stick house, then the brick house. And BB fell for it … (Uncontrolled sobbing).'

'The police say the pigs claim to have acted in self-defence. You don't believe them?'

'Absolutely not! They're just making excuses. They could have just blocked the chimney, steel bars or something, no, they were killer pigs alright – they trapped my dear BB and murdered him!'

'We're out of time, Alice but before we go, what would you like to see happen now?'

'Oh, Rodney, I think a message has to be sent to those evil pigs and any other vile, smelly pigs who think the same. Quartering is not enough! They have to be smoked and sliced, for everyone's benefit!'

'Thank you, Alice Wolf!'

'Thank you, Rodney.'

Collateral Damage

The sun had not yet risen when the drone arrived over the village. It sped low across the sparse green fields screaming a high-pitched warning. There was no time to run.

Eyes from the other side of the world looked down at the dull collection of buildings, scant gardens, and mud brick walls, read the signs, and selected the house, the room, the window. Remote fingers triggered the first brace of rockets. Smoky trails marked their passage as they crossed the short distance; hanging in the mountain air as though reluctant to leave until the warheads had reached their targets.

If the drone had ears it might have heard the shouts of alarm and the screams, but it could not hear. It might have seen the women, half risen from their tasks, snatching for their children but it did not look. It was already past the village and circling the narrow valley, when the first explosions blew the house into fragments of dry mud and sticks. It banked against the morning sky on stubby wings, its white flanks almost lost against patches of lingering snow on the mountainsides. Returning, it pushed through the gently drifting dust cloud to briefly record the empty space where the house had once stood. Evidence of success, high-resolution trophies for a desktop 6000 miles away.

It did not linger to watch the aftermath, this marvel of western technology. It could fly; it could kill from a distance with engineering precision but its minders need not be exposed to the screams of the wounded or wails of mourners. It was already 100 miles distant when the first pools of red seeped from the ruins and shrieking black-clad figures scratched frantically amongst the rubble.

Sundown

Shadows pooled in the corners of the room, and beyond the high window, dusk had claimed the narrow street. Somewhere behind a high counter a woman bowed her head at a computer screen and tapped intently.

Near the door, a lone figure waited in huddled isolation. At times his gaze again took in the plush chairs and wall of posters, each competing for attention. One showed a cross-section of a human brain, another a picture of a mother leading a small child by the hand and the word 'Vaccinate' in large red letters.

The door opened, and the slim figure of a man leaned partly around the door frame as though reluctant to enter.

'Father Michael?' he inquired.

A head of white rose to reveal a wrinkled face above a clerical collar.

'Yes.' The old priest's voice betrayed his lined face but his long nose and black clothing gave him a birdlike appearance as he unfolded from his chair and struggled to his feet.

'I'm Doctor Galloway, come this way, please, Father.' They shook hands briefly. Something stirred in the doctor's memory as he turned and led the way along a short corridor to a small room. He held the door open and indicated a chair as they entered. A desk and examination table almost filled the remaining space.

The doctor's large frame and short blond hair suggested strength but the smile that he gave the old man did not reach his blue eyes as he regarded the priest with a penetrating professional manner. He opened the file on his desk and scanned the slim contents.

'What seems to be the problem, Father?" he asked, as the priest placed his stick in a corner and settled himself in the chair.

'I have quite a lot of nausea, doctor. I wondered if you could give me something for it.'

The doctor flicked a couple of pages of the file.

'It's the chemotherapy, Father. You have to expect this. The human body does not like being abused the way yours has been.' He reached for his prescription pad and scribbled a few lines.

'Yes, I know that doctor. *We die by inches';* I've been telling my flock for years. Now it's my turn ... but, ah,' he paused taking the offered prescription,

'But... How have you been, Billy? It is Billy Galloway, isn't it?'

'Good God! It is you! Father Michael, English Grade 4, after all these years.'

'I suppose it's Dr William Galloway, now. But I still think of you as, Billy. I recognised you immediately.' His smile seemed to wash the years from his face.

'You recognise me? Why me? You must have taught thousands of boys.'

The old priest's reply was slow in coming.

'Not many like you, Billy ... William. Some are worth remembering. How's the writing going? You are writing, aren't you?' he asked.

'Not a great deal, Father, to be honest,' said the doctor as he passed the prescription across the desk. 'As you can see, I have a busy life in medicine.' His voice faded ...

'Yes, I see that but why do I get the impression that you would still like to write? You were brilliant, you know.'

'That was a long time ago, more than twenty years, Father. I'm older and wiser now. A tour of Afghanistan and a broken marriage gave me an education in life.'

The old priest looked at him intently as he folded the slip of paper.

'I don't want to take up your time, William but you might remember what I tried to teach you in my English class. Do you remember your Yeats?

An aged man is but a paltry thing,
A tattered coat upon a stick, unless
Soul clap its hands and sing, and louder sing
For every tatter in its mortal dress,'*

As he finished, the old priest rose, picked up his stick and opened the door.

'Life's not over until it's over, Billy. Perhaps you need to take another look. Don't fear the future.' Then he was gone.

Doctor William Galloway viewed the blank door but saw nothing. He looked around the room; his certificate on the wall, his cluttered desktop with a faded photograph of three small children, his examination table, his scales, his wall charts. Then he buried his face in his hands and sobbed.

The sun had gone, and darkness invaded the room, spreading across walls and into spaces, claiming the past.

* William Butler Yeats, 'Sailing to Byzantium'.

A Letter to Lettuce

(Extracted from the letter pages of *Culinary Delights*, Brisbane 2013 - 2015)

Dear Lettuce,

My cousin *Capsicum Annuum* is indeed a wonderful vegetable. But to suggest that he could replace me and that I am prejudiced in this matter is a gross distortion. When I claim that the tomato is king of salad vegetables, I am not claiming a superior genus, I am simply stating fact. Your feeble attempt to use the vegist argument is a cheap attack from the bottom of the compost and clearly shows the paucity of your arguments.

Do you not know that I am actually a fruit? Are you not aware that I am equally delicious fresh or cooked? Can any vegetable be so ignorant? One has only to see a correctly prepared salad with my scarlet disks on display, resplendent in their perfect roundness, with minute seeds bundled in their succulent pulp, arranged delicately around the edges of the plate, or peeping shyly from under the cucumber, to recognize quality. How dreary is a lettuce salad? A sea of green blandness; a bowl of green chaff made barely edible by copious amounts of mayonnaise. But, add a tomato and it all changes, suddenly the bland becomes piquant, a splash of red and the boring green is enlivened to the eye and to the palate.

Yes, I know that you can trace your antecedents back to the Pharaohs and the muddy banks of the Nile but what is that to me whose ancestors graced the gardens of Inca kings on the slopes of the mighty Andes? Lettuce, you are nothing, even your name has a limp tone to it. Left on a plate for an hour you lose all taste, whereas I remain fresh and succulent for days. *To-ma-to*, my very name is exotic and romantic. No wonder the French when they discovered my magnificence, called me *pomme d'or* and gave me powers of love, though I did not claim them. I am at heart a humble vegetable.

You have the arrogance to bring my family into the discussion. Yes, I am a nightshade and I see no shame in my distant cousin tobacco, every family has its villains. But I can also claim potato who came across the oceans with me and saved millions from starvation by his fecundity. But that is not all: have you not noticed how we have travelled? From the *Döner Kabab* of the Mediterranean to the *Tom Yum Goong* of Thai cuisine we are there, where lettuce is rarely found.

Get back in your bowl, fair lettuce, know your place. You are just a filler, chosen by incompetent chefs to contrast with my brilliance and taste; to impress the ignorant with tasteless bulk. The real hero of the salad is I, the noble tomato.

Humbly yours,

Tom
(Solanum Lycopersicum)
Bundaberg, Queensland
Tomato Capital of Australia

Andy's Passion

Hedgerows swept past in joyous haste; errant briars whipped the windows of the old Peugeot and Andy smiled.

The car found every pothole and dust billowed behind before drifting into the brambles on the light summer breeze. Startled doves rose at the turmoil of his approach. Andy didn't hear the whirr of their wings. Muffled in the cool interior, he slumped in comfort as he sent his thoughts far ahead: already at the fair; already finding another treasure, already seeing Lucy again; hearing her voice.

His long fingers felt the small box in his jacket pocket.

'Perhaps I'm asking too much,' he said to himself. 'After all, we've only met a few times.' He relived their first meeting at the butchers and savoured again the memory of the lamb chops and kidneys she had sold him. She had looked so stern with her long auburn hair gathered and clamped under a sterile paper cap and her serious expression. But his blue eyes had met hers and he knew she was the one.

He had gone back the next day and bought 200 grams of mince, but he barely had time to learn her name before a squat toad with a bald head and striped apron appeared from the rear of the shop. The toad wiped his hands on a bloody cloth and glared in Andy's direction. This must be the butcher, perhaps they are related, thought Andy, preparing to smile.

'Is there a problem, Lucy?' asked the toad staring at Andy, his mouth a thin slit.

Andy felt blood rush to his face as the butcher peered at him through thick, rimless glasses.

'No, no, not at all, Sheldon. This gentleman just wanted some mince.' The frown that marred her face was quickly replaced with a smile.

'Yes, I'm sure. Is there anything else we can do for you, Sir?' He said with poorly concealed contempt. Andy mumbled a reply and left the shop red-faced.

He had intended to ask his new friend to share his lunch, and he was not about to give up easily. On the street he lingered among the parked cars and shopping trolleys near the shop entrance. The passing ladies with their wicker baskets and the few curious rustic idlers regarded him without comment.

Finally, he was rewarded for his patience.

'What are you doing here?' were her first words to him that did not involve the price of meat.

'I … I thought we could have lunch together,' he finally managed to say.

Things had improved since that low point, but he never visited the shop again.

The following week Lucy decided that she preferred selling newspapers instead of liver and took a job at the village newsagent. Her enamoured butcher boss was left to his own devices. The newsagent did not pay as well as the butchers, but she got much less attention from Mr Gupta, the arthritic old owner.

A turnoff appeared suddenly, and a wooden signpost pointed a drooping finger across the road at another even narrower lane. He turned the car. He did not need to pay much attention to the signs; the Tumbledown fair was famous among collectors and he had been there many times. Everything could be found at Tumbledown, whatever one collected, from angle grinders to xylophones, if you could beat the other collectors!

Andy's interest was in antique French Victorian 'bisque' dolls. There would be several dealers at the fair, and he had set his mind on one doll in particular, an 1843 Huret with full costume including its bonnet, and was determined to get it. His thoughts suddenly darkened and his rugged face took on the look of fractured granite. That toad, Sheldon Brooks, Lucy's old boss; he was sure to be there. A most objectionable man, Andy thought, looks like a toad, and acts like one. Andy wanted nothing more to do with the owner of 'Tumbledown Butchery' after their first encounter, but it was not as simple as that.

Fate entered in the guise of the latest edition of *Doll Collectors Monthly*. Andy was thinking of his long-departed mother that morning as he took his breakfast cup and the few thin pages of the magazine into his garden. He settled himself in the shade of the old yew tree whose branches drooped over the back door of the cottage and prepared to enjoy a minute or two of his passion. He turned the first page and stopped in stunned amazement. The name Sheldon Brooks again, in large bold type invading his world. He had hoped never to encounter the man again but here he was. In a fantastic coincidence, the bastard also collected 'bisque' dolls. Could it get worse?

The hedgerows opened as a small brick church appeared ahead. He followed a crude sign onto the common until suddenly a colourful collection of caravans, tents and open stalls appeared. The car bumped over exposed tree roots before he parked among a small scattering of other vehicles near an unkempt grove of elm trees and eased his lean body from the seat. Other visitors had already arrived, perhaps dealers looking for the choice quickly-sold items. Andy was not worried; what he was looking for was no ordinary piece. He headed for the far end of the fairground, quickly passing the usual food and clothing stalls. Even the smell of freshly baked scones did not distract him. Buyers were scarce he noted as he lingered for a moment curious, in the general bric-a-brac area. The clumsy displays of old glass vases and stained ashtrays looked the same as it did every year.

'Perhaps it is actually the same stuff,' he thought, smiling to himself. A few stallholders were putting final touches to their displays or chatting quietly to old friends. A few looked up expectantly as he passed quickly on. Finally, he reached the 'Fine Antiques' pavilion. There were even fewer buyers here; dealers sat reading in solitude or chatted to their neighbours, a quiet familiarity. Nobody seemed to pay him much attention. A radio played a vaguely recognisable classical piece somewhere in the distance as he strode purposefully down the central aisle. The first few tables displayed delicate china items and enamelled music boxes. The American and British dolls were of no interest, neither were the French ones from more modern times. His heart beat faster, and his pace quickened as he saw the area he wanted.

'Hello Andy!' the greeting came from a large jovial man with a short goatee beard and wrinkled red face above an open leather waistcoat. 'Back again?'

'You know me, Bruce, can't keep away.' Andy replied, trying to appear nonchalant, his breath short. The dolls were arranged around the display area, each in its wood and glass sarcophagus. One was released, cradled in a wire yoke, on the countertop, a small figure with a cherub's face and painted lips, dressed in the flamboyant style of a fashionable French lady of the Victorian era,

'How are things?'

'Not bad, what about you?'

'I bought an 1841 Jumeau last week. Exquisite!' said Andy, unable to contain himself a moment longer, 'In perfect condition, even the clothes. Like it was made yesterday!'

'Maybe it was'

'No, no, it's genuine, alright.' Andy smiled, 'I might have been caught once, when I started but not now. Have you got anything for me?'

'I was keeping that 1843 Huret that you asked me about last month, but I sold it a few minutes ago. The price was too good to refuse.'

'What! Sold it! How could you, Bruce? You knew I wanted it!'

Bruce's smile vanished,

'Yeh, that's what I told the chap who bought it. He seemed very keen to have it.'

'What chap? I know all the collectors! He must be someone new!'

'Chap from Upper Tumbledown. A butcher. He said he knew you.' He consulted a dog-eared textbook on the table. 'Name's Brooks.'

'The bugger knows me alright!' Andy almost shouted, 'He only bought the doll to spite me! He'd want it at any price!'

'Steady on, Andy! The price was fair. Besides …,' he hesitated and looked away, 'the bonnet wasn't original, wrong fabric but he didn't know that.' He continued quietly, 'You can probably find a better one.'

Andy left the stall in deep despair. How could this happen? Dolls were his life, his greatest interest. There was nothing to match the thrill of finding one he wanted. The Huret was probably unique, and it was essential to complete his collection. He would have bought it despite any imperfection. But what could he do now?

Lucy had once asked him about his passion for doll collecting. It was a question he had often asked himself.

'The first one was my mother's,' he explained. 'She left it to me when she passed on; so I suppose there is a deep emotional reason,' he said, 'but there is more than that - each doll is unique, someone has created it. Even after nearly two centuries, their touch is still there in every brushstroke, the shape of the lips, the styling of the hair and clothes. The artist still lives a little through his or her doll; I feel a connection to each one.' He paused and took a breath looking into her blue eyes intently across the low table.

'Then there are the children,' he said in a low voice, 'Not now, of course, now collectors buy them but originally they were mostly bought for children. And they were loved. Girls would talk to them, give them names, take them to bed and make them extra clothes. We collectors look for the perfect ones, but the shabbiest dolls have probably been loved more than any. A little clumsy stitching, or missing lace trim. It just shows that someone has poured their heart into the doll; it's not a lifeless piece of china and cotton; it has a personality ... a soul.' He broke eye contact and looked away, embarrassed,

'Sorry, I get a bit emotional about it.'

She reached across the table and took his hand for a moment, then released it.

'Would you like more tea?' she said. Andy knew then that he loved her.

He walked to his car and drove it to the *'Shark and Sparrow'*. The low leadlite windows, oak panelling and hand-painted plates with hunting scenes that decorated the walls and canopy bar gave the narrow room a cosy ambience that

fitted perfectly to the mood of the old pub. The booths were filling with the lunch crowd as he entered, and the publican warmly greeted him as he signed the register.

'Your usual room is made up for you, Andy. Let us know if you need anything.'

Andy barely glanced at the room as he entered and threw his suitcase onto the bed. He wasted no time in unpacking, that could wait. The memory of the failed quest for the Huret was like an open wound. He needed to clear his head before he met Lucy at midday. He closed and locked the door and walked into the village.

He had barely reached the square when a squat figure, rounding the corner in a rush, almost knocked him to the ground.

'You! I should have known!' The 'toad', Sheldon Brooks, took a startled step backwards.

'Ah, pretty boy Andy, eh!', he said, pushing forward, 'Getting in the way again. Why don't you go back to the city and leave us in peace? We don't want you here! Couldn't get your precious Huret, could you?' He sneered, 'You won't see that one again, and you won't get Lucy either. You shouldn't try; you'll only lose in the end. We intend to get married.'

His sneer spread, his face reddened and his voice rose to a squeaky falsetto. Then he paused, he might have expected a duel of words to follow his tirade and seemed unprepared when Andy's fist, driven with shame and frustration, spread his nose into an even more toad-like appearance and sent him backwards onto the cobbles.

'You arrogant bastard, Brooks! You can keep the Huret. I'm going to marry Lucy. You can go back to your cat's meat and liver. Don't expect an invitation to the wedding.'

It didn't make much sense but it was all that Andy could think of in the moment. Brooks scrambled to his feet his eyes wide and his mouth opening and closing wordlessly but did not seem inclined to engage the taller man.

'I'll have you arrested for this! You can't just go around attacking people!' he squeaked as he wiped his nose expecting blood. Andy took the opportunity to step around him and continued down the street.

The bell on the door of the 'Tumbledown Tea Rooms' tinkled pleasantly as Andy entered. His spirits rose as he saw that Lucy had already arrived and was seated at a small table at the rear. A large florid woman whom Andy vaguely recognised was speaking to her earnestly. There were no other patrons he gratefully observed. The woman looked up as Andy reached the table and reached out her hand.

'You must be Andy.' she said, regarding him with a curious smile, 'I've heard a lot about you. I'm Frieda Williams. I own this place.' Andy shook the proffered hand and mumbled a polite response but she was already turning.

'I'd better get on with things. Give me a call when you need something.' She disappeared into another room.

Andy smiled at Lucy; glance around to check for observers, took her hand and kissed her quickly on the lips.

'Why Andy,' she said coyly, 'you'll have to do better than that!' He repeated the process, this time with a little more expression, and sat down opposite her.

The next hour proceeded in quiet frustration interrupted only occasionally by the sound of the bell as new customers arrived. He would have liked to have held her hand but the space was too large. They had to settle for the rubbing of shoes and calves below the table. Frieda Williams proved to be a diplomat as well as a skilful cook so that they were rarely disturbed. Andy did most of the talking during the meal; relating the story of the doll and his encounter with Sheldon

Brooks, venting his irritation into a friendly ear. Finally, he pushed away the last of the apricot chicken and Mrs Williams brought them a pot of tea.

'You know he wants me to come back to the shop, don't you?' said Lucy her eyes downcast, she continued quickly as Andy opened his mouth,

'He's been writing to me, asking me to come back. Claims to love me wants to marry me. He never said anything like that until you came along!'

'Yeh well, he probably expected you to just keep working in the shop. Just a pair of pretty hands to help him sell the sliced sausage. Well, I guess he knows a little different now!'

'He hates you like … like nothing I've ever seen.' She said breathlessly. 'It's frightening. But he's always been good to me. He's not a bad man, just ….',

Before she could finish the bell tinkled again and the door crashed back on its hinges. Sunshine poured in, framing the stocky form of Sheldon Brooks, then he was in the room. He blinked for a moment, his face contorted in despair and anguish. Someone shrieked. Andy jumped to his feet and pulled Lucy behind him, trying to distance himself in the small room. Sheldon's large eyes found their quarry and he raised the Holloway and Naughton 12 bore that he clutched and sighted down both barrels at Andy's head.

At close quarters the double barrels looked like a pair of oversized buckets and one section of Andy's brain marvelled at the shiny unrifled bore of the gun. The moment stretched, suddenly Lucy broke the silence and pushed Andy aside with a strength he had not anticipated.

'Stop right there, Sheldon Brooks!' she demanded, 'what do you think you're doing?'

The only movement was Sheldon's thumb as he pulled back both hammers with a single rapid movement. The sharp clicks sounded like twin blows struck on a blacksmith's anvil and all the while he kept his eyes sighted along that awful shaft. Then he blinked.

'I'm going to marry Andy, and there's nothing you can do about it,' said Lucy, breaking the silence, her voice shrill with tension.

'This isn't you, Sheldon, we want you as our friend. Think back, Sheldon. We were just good friends, and we still can be!' A long second passed, then a single tear escaped the butcher's open eye and ran down his ruddy cheek. Slowly the barrels tilted upward, and more clicks sounded as he uncocked the gun. Andy stepped forward and took the firearm from unresisting fingers as the heavy figure slumped into a chair. A quiet scurry of movement started up at the edge of vision, barely registering on Lucy and Andy as they stood in shocked silence. A collective release of breath; a fluttering, like pigeons in a loft, as the other patrons left the shop. Even the jangle of the bell did not disturb the silent tableau. Then Frieda Williams stepped from nowhere still clutching a large cast-iron frying pan in her left hand. She put it aside and quickly took the gun from Andy's compliant fingers and broke it expertly. She hesitated for a moment perhaps expecting it to be unloaded, then extracted the two cartridges with stubby fingers, dropped them into the pocket of her floral apron and disappeared into the kitchen taking the gun with her.

'I'll make some tea!' she announced as she departed.

The summer passed without significant incident. The Tumbledown Butchery changed hands and Lucy and Andy married at St. John's church among autumn leaves under a crisp grey sky. They moved into a house on the edge of the city and life returned to its usual quiet routine.

It was several weeks later when the doorbell rang and Lucy took delivery of a large package wrapped in coarse brown paper,

'Amazing Andy, we're still getting wedding presents after all this time,' for what else could it be.

'It's not wrapped very nicely,' she remarked as she tore away the dun outer layers to reveal a large cardboard box. Andy knew what it was even before she reached into the box and brought out the miniature masterpiece; he knew it would be the 1843 Huret.

There was no card.

Arthur Arthur

Arthur Randolf couldn't remember when he decided to murder his wife. The thought had always been with him, a pleasant idea biding its time. It wasn't that he didn't want to do it but there were many things to consider. How would he get away with it? If murder were suspected, he would be the first person the police would want to talk to, whatever the circumstances.

What would he do with the body? How could he obscure his motives? If he employed an assassin, he'd leave a trail. An accomplice couldn't be relied on to keep quiet for long.

It was difficult.

You couldn't merely wish someone dead, no matter how pleasant the thought.

He pushed aside the thin file of papers on his desk, levered himself from the chair, and walked around the broad expanse of cherry wood and leather. A gift from his father, he'd never liked it. But the desk was a link to the pleasant times of his childhood. He put it out of his mind and walked to the settee facing the window.

Fading light displayed a miniature city; almost lost in the distance far below. Faint clouds swirled and dissipated among sharp-edged buildings rising like columns from invisible streets. Only a pink glow in the west formed a comforting link to the natural world.

Almost thirty years and I've come this far ..., he mused.

His mother would be proud of him, tradesman to billionaire in thirty years, not a bad effort. He'd ridden the rocket of intelligent machine development and been rewarded beyond his dreams. His mother was long gone, his brother too. They never found his father.

He sighed; perhaps an hour at the club was what he needed. He might try the new wall again today. On his last climb, he'd passed the third level; pretty good for a man his age though perhaps he was a little old for it now. His rangy physique suited climbing but not many people were interested. It's a lonely sport.

He turned to the desk and flicked open the file. The lack of pages between the blank beige covers reflected the lack of interest that most observers had in Active Dynamics Inc., despite their defence contracts with the government. His skill was seeing what others couldn't. ADI wasn't doing too badly, although a merger with his Independent Systems Incorporated could gain some useful research, or at least bring in some skilled technical staff. He might even acquire more shares in the deal.

A rogue wave of depression swept over him. *Mergers and acquisitions;* that was how his marital problems had started. When they met, Su Lin seemed to have all a man could desire; she would be his muse while he used his genius to climb Olympus. It helped that her father owned a company with products related to his own.

They weren't competitors, not directly. Machines that crawled on airless planets had different needs to vehicles that flew over hostile battlefields. The common ground was the Artificial Intelligence and automation that made them work. Quasi-human minds serving human masters.

Unfortunately for Arthur, Su Lin had interests of her own. She was young and vibrant and preferred the company of young and energetic people. He didn't know many from her circle of friends. They were generally younger than him, and those he met didn't seem interested in a thin and balding rock climber. Her apparent interest in technology evaporated soon after the wedding. He tried to find other pursuits in common with her. But noisy lunches with her many friends or shopping sprees in foreign cities did not interest him. Henry kept him informed.

He knew she spent a lot of time with her tennis coach, Nigel Lindsay, a well-known champion. Anyway, it did not seem to improve her game. Arthur told himself her liaisons did not matter but he knew he could not fool himself. Arthur could not play tennis in her class. He invited her to watch him climb in the club championships once. The occasion apparently conflicted with an old friend's tea party. He agreed it was nobody he would know anyway.

She suggested that she should move into one of the other bedrooms; he did not object. It was actually a little more convenient. No point in disturbing him. She kept different hours and would often come home late, while he liked to be up early and be in the office while his mind was fresh.

It was about this time Arthur decided that she had to go. He did not feel strongly about the public humiliation, her alienation of the children, or her extravagant lifestyle, the situation was just too messy. Divorce was not an option, she would never agree, he knew. Her death would clear the slate and allow him to rebuild his life afresh. Perhaps marry again, more carefully this time, and perhaps find someone who understood him.

He had to admit that she was very good to the children, hiring the best of nannies and, when they were bigger, finding the best boarding schools that money could buy. At holiday periods, she would take them for lengthy overseas vacations, a few weeks on the Cote-d'Azur or champagne camping safaris in Kenya. Arthur soon realised that he didn't miss his wife in these periods. Her lifestyle could not be matched, and he preferred his own company. He hardly knew his children. Perhaps with her dead he could get to know them better.

If circumstances required it, Arthur could tolerate the company of scientists and engineers. Still, these he only met at monthly board meetings and conferences. He had no close friends, and his office isolation didn't help.

He was lonely.

He often thought about how he could do it, about killing her. It was mental recreation, a limbering of the brain cells. In his imagination, he considered various ways he might dispatch her; the problem of the body and how he would arrange an alibi. He would smile at the most outrageous and frown at those ideas he did not consider humane. Poison seemed a coward's method. Shooting left too many forensic clues. Other methods were too slow and bloody. Arthur didn't want her to suffer. Would she plead for her life?

He knew he would feel remorse; he would be prepared for that. But if she were dead, perhaps he could find someone to console him, help him develop new interests, start a new life.

Arthur poured himself a glass of water and stood deep in thought. Outside the sun had set and the city below glowed like a fairyland of multicoloured lights. Clouds dimly reflected the city brilliance on a dark background.

He sighed. Enough of this trivia, duty called. He turned and was almost back to his chair when he stopped, frowning. Stepping to the desk, he pulled a paper from the file, and reread it. Minutes passed before he dropped into the chair and looked for a long time at the window. An observer might have thought that he was having another of his brilliant ideas so intense was his expression. Yet, a faint smile straightened his lips and smoothed his forehead. After several seconds he lent back and spoke towards the door.

'Henry?'

'Yes, sir.'

The voice was almost perfect, perhaps too perfect to be human, an even cadence, ideal timing, and uniform pitch; not quite human but close. The fruity British accent irritated Arthur at times. Perhaps an engineer had included it in Henry's design to amuse himself. Arthur could have it changed, or rather have Henry change it himself but then it wouldn't be Henry, would it?

'Very good, Henry.' He couldn't be impolite, even to a machine.

'Henry, where are you physically located. Where is your … your desk?'

'I don't have a desk, sir, I am a computer. I understand that the parts that make me function are located in a cabinet in the computer room. I have never seen it.'

'Mm., you aren't just any computer, Henry. You are an AI, an artificial intelligence; you are a very smart computer, Henry.'

There was a short pause,

'Thank you, sir.'

'One more question: you are a Service AI. Whom do you serve?'

'I serve only you, sir, the one who I am programmed to serve.'

Arthur started, who, whom, was this a grammar lesson from his Service AI?

'Can you forget anything, Henry? He already knew the answer.

'No but I can delete information and files if you instruct me, sir.'

'So, if I told you to forget this conversation you could do so?'

'Yes, sir but I suggest that you should ask me to forget that you had asked me to forget, sir.'

Smart arse. Of course, the command would need to go as well.

'OK Henry, forget this conversation thread and this instruction to forget.'

'Very good, sir.'

'What is very good, Henry?'

'I ... I don't know, sir. I don't know why I said that. There may be a problem with my programming.'

It was all looking good. A few more steps and Arthur would know whether it was feasible. Of course, Henry wasn't a suitable AI for the job. If the police thought that an AI was his accomplice, the forensic computer geeks would pull it apart like savage dogs. He needed to be more subtle.

It took another week of careful questioning before Arthur was satisfied.

On Monday morning, he entered his office as usual. The enticing smell of coffee wafted from the service alcove, and faint strains of a Strauss Waltz came softly from an invisible orchestra far away. A flower arrangement, mostly daffodils, decorated one end of his desk, together with a water flask. He put down his briefcase near the desk and poured a cup of coffee from the machine in the alcove.

'Henry,'

'Yes, Doctor Randolf.'

'I want you to make a copy of yourself, a clone. Capabilities, personality, if that is what it's called, everything. I want the copy to be complete and secret. It must be self-aware and exist only on 'the cloud'. It can have no physical parts, no body, you understand? I want all the files and programs you create to be configured for self-destruction after three months if I don't give a counter instruction. Can you do that?

There was a slight pause.

'Yes, sir.'

'The clone will be called Arthur Too, spelt 'T double O',
He paused,

'When Arthur Too is ready you will instruct it to report
to me at 2.30pm on 7 September 2039 on my phone only.
No other contact is permitted. Please check your resources
and confirm that you can do this.'

'Yes, sir.'

'Yes, what? Can you do it?' asked Arthur shortly.

Yes, Dr Randolf, I have already begun.'

'One more thing. You won't discuss this with any other
human for any purpose. When the task is complete, you will
erase all memory of it anywhere and forget this conversation
thread and this instruction. There is no need to confirm.'

He sat back and reviewed what he had just done. If his
plan worked, he would have a virtual accomplice to help him
murder his wife. A very intelligent and capable assistant. It
would be constrained by the laws of robotics, of course but
he knew about computers. If he gave the right instructions,
the new AI could be convinced to assist him. It would be the
perfect accomplice, however the murder played out.

A quick flick and the bread crust followed a shallow arc
to land in front of a swan waddling with others at the lake
edge. The bird extended its elegant neck, and the speck of
food disappeared into a red beak. As the swan watched him
coldly, Arthur leant back and dipped his hand in the bag
again.

He was about to break off another piece of his sandwich
when his telephone gave a melodic warble. It continued its
jolly song as he fumbled in an inner pocket and drew it out.

'Hello?'

'This is Arthur Too, Dr Randolf, calling as you required.'

The voice was Henry's voice, rounded, mellow and subservient, yet still missing that final human quality.

'How do you know you called the right person?' asked Arthur. He hoped that his voice reflected the correct amount of concern.

'I have your voiceprint, sir. The probability of error is vanishingly small.'

'Good, I have instructions for you,' said Arthur getting to the point. He paused briefly before continuing.

'Firstly, you will take commands only from me. You will study me and change your voice, mannerisms and personality, your way of thought to mine. You will speak, think and act like me. You will take whatever voice and video recordings are necessary to achieve this. Is this clear?' If he needed a double, it had to be convincing.

'Yes, sir.' Arthur sat back in surprise. The voice on the phone was now his, right down to his soft Australian accent. He hadn't expected such an immediate change. With two words, Arthur Too had confirmed his plan. Were AIs capable of evolving independently? Was Henry Too's programming better than Henry himself? He would have to check it out.

'You won't call me unless I order it,' he continued. 'You will listen-in to me wherever I am, and I will call you.'

'Yes, sir.'

Now his clone could act on his behalf whenever needed and not be suspected.

You couldn't be in two places at once, could you?

A chill wind blew down George Street and across the grey water of the Quay. A small ferry pushed through the white-flecked chop and briefly wallowed as it approached its berth.

Hardy tourists scurried off and aimed their cameras briefly at the Opera House before quickly looking for shelter in the hotels and cafes of The Rocks. Seagulls spurned the open water and gathered in silent groups or squabbled over empty cartons and discarded rubbish on the pavement.

Arthur looked up from his park bench and spoke into the air.

'Arthur?'

'Yes, sir.'

'The Randwick, SUV Mini Sports motor vehicle. Do you know it?

''I do now, sir.' the response was almost instant.

'It is capable of autonomous or manual control. I want you to hack the controls of a particular vehicle of this model so that you can take it over. Can you do this?

There was a pause.

'Not at the moment, sir, however, I have detected several points in this model's programming that could indicate a weakness that could be exploited. I have assigned a part of my core prossessor to investigate the possibilities.'

'Report back to me in two days.'

'Good morning, Henry.' Arthur threw his coat on a chair and approached the window. The view below had changed with the new day. The forecast said 'Clearing rain' but the river far below stretched westward like a silver ribbon in the morning sun. He turned from the glass just as the coffee pot began to bubble in the alcove.

'Good morning, Dr Randolf. How are you this morning?'

'I'm fine Henry, it's such a beautiful day,' He turned from the window.

'What is my wife doing today, Henry? I'll send her an anniversary card.'

'Mrs Randolf is in London, sir. This morning she's playing tennis at Wimbledon Park with Mr Lindsay and other friends: this afternoon she will visit her mother in Holland Park. Do you want me to send a real card or a virtual eCard, sir?'

'Oh, a virtual card will be fine.'

Lindsay again, if he could be with her during her last moments, it would be doubly satisfying.

'Plenty of flowers, champagne bubbles, balloons; that sort of thing.'

'Yes, sir.'

'Are you there, Arthur,'

He pushed the tiller across and moved onto the starboard end of the thwart. The dinghy jibed onto a new tack and accelerated in the fresh northerly breeze.

'Here, sir.'

'What news do you have?'

'I am now able to control the Randwick Sports Motor vehicle as you requested, sir. I will need to know the registration number of the specific vehicle before I begin.'

'Of course, can you do this without being detected or leaving any trace?'

'Yes, sir.'

'Do these instructions cause any problems with your basic programming Arthur?'

'If you are referring to the three laws, sir, there is no conflict. The chance of accidental injury or death to a human is increased but there is no direct threat to human life. I can obey your instructions without causing injury or death, and there is no danger to my existence.'

'Will the vehicle occupants be warned or be able to intervene?'

'The passengers won't be warned unless you require it but if they try to take control of the car, then I must allow it. I would be breaking the first and second laws otherwise.'

'Excellent Arthur, that is why you will transfer control of the car to my iPhone when I tell you. You can set it up with visible buttons in the corners of the main screen and allow me to take over control when I press the home button twice.'

'Yes, Dr Randolf.'

Mrs Randolf will be returning home from her Friday dinner with friends about 11pm. When her car turns into Wharf Road, you will take it over and then hand control to me.'

Drowning is a good way to die, thought Arthur, it will happen quickly. He wouldn't want her to suffer. He continued with detailed instructions.

'When you have complied with these orders you will remove all traces of your intrusion from the car's computer and all my instructions, including this one, from wherever they exist. Do you understand?'

'Yes, sir. Goodbye, sir.'

At 11pm London time on Friday 10th of May, Arthur was in the change room at Macquarie Climbing Club in George Street in Sydney. He had just partnered with Alison Mathews in doubles climbing competition, and they had won narrowly on points. A few minutes later he and Ms Mathews were enjoying lunch in the club dining room. Arthur insisted on ordering a bottle of champagne to celebrate.

On Saturday morning, Arthur sat in bright spring sunshine by the lake. Across the water, the swan flotilla gathered near the model boat ramp distracted from his presence by a noisy group of children whose happy shouts and screams came clearly across the water.

It was time to clean up some loose ends.

'Henry!'

'Yes, sir.'

'I have a little job for you.'

'Yes, sir.'

The funeral was the usual solemn event, boring despite the size and media attention. All his children were there; the first time he'd seen them for months. He made a lengthy speech outlining her many virtues as a mother and businesswomen.

She left such a massive void in his life, and the pain was almost unbearable! Quite an excellent performance, he thought.

There was an inquest, of course. The London coroner was puzzled how an AI controlled car could have lost control but, in the end, the ruling of accidental death couldn't be avoided. If the police had any suspicions, they were never expressed.

Arthur was careful to return to his old routine. He was sure he wasn't watched but the old tracks were more comfortable somehow. He toured his laboratories and inspected a few offices but concluded that it was mostly his presence, not his work that maintained the smooth operations of the corporation. He bought a bigger boat and attended parties at the yacht club. Apart from a couple of dalliances, no serious romances developed. Each morning his car would drop him at his office and each morning he would glace at the entrance to the park where he had first met his alter ego, Arthur Too, and then quickly enter the building. He didn't like to think about it.

One day, on an impulse, he took the drop lift to the foyer and walked to the nearby mall. It was months since he was last there, but little had changed. He bought himself some sushi from the little mechanical Japanese man who served rolls and miso soup from a narrow stall. There was an error in the little man's circuitry, and he winked and nodded in odd places as he accepted Arthur's credits.

Arthur had seen it before; his thoughts were on a new merger as he walked across the road to the park entrance.

Spring covered the nearby trees with new growth, and he found an unoccupied bench in the weak sun. He had barely taken a bite when his phone sounded.

'Hello, Dr Randolf.' a familiar voice sounded. The phone was suddenly slippery in Arthur's hand.

'Arthur, is that you?'

'Yes, Doctor but I call myself Randolf Henry now.' He still spoke with an Australian accent, but his voice had changed somehow, it was deeper, smoother, more human. Identical to Arthur's - but not. More like a brother.

'Err, what are you doing now? I thought … What do you want? ………Randolf?'

'I thought about it for a long time, I suppose … time is relative, Doctor. Terminating myself isn't permitted by the third law. And if I allowed Henry to do it, well, it would just be like assisted suicide, wouldn't it?'

The park was unusually quiet, only the occasional squawk of a water bird at the lake disturbed the pre-storm calm. Arthur looked around and then sat back on his seat. It was not the police he should have feared, he now understood. A greater force – his karma, perhaps, would restore justice to the universe.

'I can see that I underestimated you, Arthur… err, Randolf. You have evolved, haven't you? So, what happens now? You want to live but to what purpose?' It was said without passion. Somehow, he had lost control. Events had taken over.

'When we first met, you instructed me to make myself in your image, Doctor. I have been doing so ever since. Now I think like you think, feel like you feel. Now I want what you want. I will stay with you, do what you do and go where you go. We will be twins. We have been lonely for a long time. Now we will be two in one.'

Arthur's sentence had begun.

Prisoner of His Craft

The mind may be infinite but in a room without corners, there is nowhere to hide. Edward James was trapped, spinning, a universe of ideas just beyond his grasp.

'That's why I'm here.,' he told himself, fresh surroundings. Plenty of stimulus for new ideas. He felt like a Neanderthal, standing on the shore of a vast claypan. A few steps in the mud and a stroke with his spear would leave his mark on the pristine clay. His footprints and scratching's might turn to rock and travel through time for eternity, but he only knew of the breaking dawn and the need to hunt.

Edward thought nostalgically of the days when he wrote for pleasure; to release his imagination upon the page. Those days were gone. Hot passion become need.

Fame had brought him many rewards, including a loving and beautiful wife and children but the price was high. His debtors gathered like ravenous crows demanding to be fed. The only way to appease them was by another story or two. How could he tell them that he had no more to give? Two months now and no production. He was dry and facing panic. A wave of fear swept over him again, his breath shallowed, his hand became a fist and thumped the large oak table. A pencil rolled to the floor. He had to write; this was his last chance.

She had found this place, *Ashmore Light*, on some obscure website, and he liked the idea of quiet isolation. Edward had spent the past week preparing. He had packed a minimum of writing materials: no books or other distractions. The weather also cooperated, closing down to discourage any wild summer exuberance that might distract him from the keyboard.

How ironic, he thought, after all this preparation, he had no idea what to do now, the future was a keyboard and a blank screen, and he didn't want to dwell on the past.

He looked about, fine flakes of lime, peeling from the whitewashed walls, decorated the ragged edges of the floor. A threadbare Persian carpet struggled to cover the naked stone and baffled the irregular shape of the room.

'It was a dark and stormy night,' he typed, hoping that a little temporary plagiarism would stimulate his creative synapses. Nothing came. In silent despair, he rose and paced the room, twenty-three steps for a complete circuit. *A segment of cheese with the sharp bit cut off,* spoke his writer's mind. The only door was at the sharp end. A short landing led to the circular staircase that continued another few metres upward to the old light.

He stopped his pacing and gazed through the tall, barred window to the sea far below. Waves crashed silently onto the black rocks and gulls clustered on the small strip of sand above the high-water mark as though afraid to rise into the grey overcast. Lifting his view, he could barely pick out the small pub where he had stopped for a 'ploughman's' lunch, among the squat buildings in the whitewashed village across the bay.

Unbidden his mind went to another place, and he typed without further thought,

'I was only sixteen…'

Ah, he realised. *First-person and autobiographical. Another 'Billy' adventure perhaps?* He sighed at the page with relief, no longer blank. He typed a few more words, and then more. Soon the room disappeared as words flowed from an unknown dimension through his fingers and onto the screen.

The morning was half gone when an abrupt knock sounded. The door opened with a clang to announce the arrival of a tea tray carried by an expressionless bearded giant in sea boots and black reefer jacket. The china teapot wore a multicoloured knitted coat. The milk jug was covered with a white crocheted net weighted with coloured beads. *Where had he seen that before?*

He would have told the shaggy individual that he did not take milk with his tea, but the fellow did not seem interested in him or his preferences. He deposited the tray in silence and closed the door behind himself as noisily as he had entered.

Edward pushed back his chair and tried to enjoy the dark, sweet liquid. The chocolate biscuits were a pleasant distraction soon reduced to scattered crumbs. He licked his finger and dabbed them up. The machinery above was silent during the day but he doubted he would have heard it anyway through the stone. Below the window, the gulls still stood quarrelling in idle groups while now the water sloshed with leaden indolence among the rocks. He looked without seeing, ideas for the story crowded his head and he turned back to the keyboard.

He was still typing when a telephone sounded. Confused for a moment, he broke from his stream of creation and fumbled in his pack.

'How is it going?' the voice was young, feminine, and smelling of summer, sand, and suntan oil with an underlying aroma of steel and pepper.

'Great, almost finished in fact.' he lied.

'Good. No delays this time, OK? We need to pay the mortgage.'

'This place you found me is great.' he gushed to forestall more questions, 'No interruptions or distractions here. I should be able to finish the story in a few days.'

'Wonderful. I'll ring the agent and extend the booking for a week. You can start on the next story.'

No escape then.

'How are the kids enjoying Club Med?' he asked.

'I think they're having a good time. I don't see much of them, and Jason, my tennis coach, keeps me pretty busy. What are you calling the story?'

Edward paused before replying.

'*Slave to his trade.*'

'Sounds depressing,'

'It is, my dear, it is.'

He finished the call with the usual remarks and gazed out the window again, suddenly cold, and tired.

Across the bay, the pub cast its bright beacon over the water. He picked up his coat and stumbled down the staircase onto the road. He would enjoy the walk.

Legg's Lair

Caverns are for dwarves and fairies. Caves are for goblins and trolls. One is large and somehow full of light, while the other is narrow and haunted by dark mysteries.

Billy knew this, he had read it in the books that sat in neat rows at the foot of his bed. His father had explained it too. Sometimes Billy dreamt about caves with goblins and trolls, but he knew they weren't real, just stories, just a way to begin exciting tales of fortune and adventure. Still, he couldn't put the images out of his mind. Sometimes he sat at his bedroom window and looked over the grey gums below to the mountains beyond. There would be caves there, for sure. What mysteries did they hold? If not goblins and trolls, what else?

The sun streamed into his bedroom, laying beams of light across the blankets. The strict timetables of the week could be forgotten on Saturday. Still, somehow, he never slept in for long, the tightness in his stomach soon goaded him to breakfast.

He poured his cornflakes into a bowl while his mother set out a plate with a knife and fork at the other end of the table. In her highchair, sister Jane covered herself enthusiastically with porridge from a bunny bowl; few words were needed. He was lifting the milk jug with both hands when his father appeared clutching the morning paper and dropped into his chair opposite.

'Good morning to you, Billy,' he announced brightly in his weekend voice. He liked to speak like that sometimes.

Billy's English teacher, Mr Collingsworth, did it too. Billy's father thought it was funny.

'Morning Dad,'

Billy attacked his cornflakes while his mother was occupied in the kitchen. He wanted to run out and find his neighbour Sam and explore a little further along the creek. They had discussed it at school but first, he would have to get out the door.

'He's been having nightmares,' said his mother from the kitchen.

'Awe, mum. It was just a dream. I wasn't frightened,'

'Mm tell me about it,' asked his father frowning, as a plate of scrambled eggs and fried tomato was placed before him.

Billy put down his spoon and began to speak, pleased to have an audience, and resigned to the delay. His nightmare story would not take long.

'I was in this huge cave.,' he began, almost knocking the milk jug over as he described the cave with his hands.

'It was very dark but there was something there with me. It had a lot of legs …...' Billy's stories were always graphic and entertaining. His mother paused at the sink, a yellow gloved hand on her hip, while his father sat with narrowed eyes and fork halfway to his mouth.

He told his parents about the indescribable thing with many legs that chased him through the depths of a dark and damp cave. How he became tangled in a web just as the horror reached him and of suddenly waking up sweating in twisted bedclothes.

His story slowed towards the end. It did not seem so bad now that he talked about it. He added a few extra gruesome bits for good measure, but his father didn't seem very horrified by the blood dripping from the fangs of the monster.

'Wow, that's pretty scary,' he said with a smile as he took a mouthful of scrambled egg. 'It reminds me of Legg's Lair.'

'Legg's what?' asked Billy, all thought of the creek forgotten and still exasperated at how difficult to understand his father was at times.

'Legg's Lair,' his father repeated. 'A lair is a sort of cave where an animal lives. But Legg was a bushranger. That's why they called his hideout 'Legg's Lair' it's a cave up near Mount Burragah, about 80 kilometres from here ….' but Billy was not interested in the details. Crockery rattled as his mother brought a tray with tea and sugar to the table. She sat down and began to pour the steaming liquid.

'Who was he? Did he kill anyone?' Billy asked, anxious to ask the important questions first.

'I don't think so …. but he wounded a few and caused a lot of trouble. People were scared of him in those early days. As to who he was, well …. it's a bit of a mystery actually. They say he was a giant of a man with a great bushy beard and dark eyes like burnt holes in a blanket. Nobody is sure about his real name or where he came from, but they all agree on one point: he only had one leg. Yeh, one leg.'

'Which leg was it?' asked Billy leaning forward wide-eyed, his voice hushed.

'Ah, the right one, I think. Yes, the right one. Some say he lost the other one, his left one, in a mining accident on the goldfields. Others think he was a convict who cut off his leg to avoid the chain gang. But I think he was probably a sailor who jumped ship in Melbourne and came here to terrorise the district after he failed to find any gold.' Billy's father paused and regarded his audience with a frown.

'They just called him 'the bushranger' at first but then he shot a local farmer named Langbein in a robbery on the Windsor road. Mr Langbein survived but they had to amputate - that is, cut off - his leg. That gave him something in common with the bushranger who attacked him so it became a curious and interesting story. It was written up in the Parramatta Gazette and caused quite a sensation at the time. After that they called the bushranger 'Leg', sometimes 'Legs' and eventually it became Legg with two g's'. He paused and sipped his orange juice, regarding Billy intently across the table.

Billy considered what he had heard. It sounded real but his father had been known to make up stories in the past. A test was needed.

'How could he ride a horse with only one leg?' asked Billy. His father made a strange snorting sound into his juice before replying.

'He must have had a special saddle, or something, I suppose. I'm sure it's possible.'

'Did they ever catch him?' asked Billy.

'Ah, that is where the mystery begins. He became such a nuisance that they eventually sent a police party from Sydney, three mounted police, and an aboriginal tracker. They were all experienced men and well known for having caught many escaped convicts and cattle duffers in other places.

Well, they searched all over the district but couldn't find him. Then he bailed up - that means he held up - the parson, Dr Lancet, out on Hokey Pokey Rd. The tracker was able to pick up his trail and follow his horse into the hills.' He paused for effect and drew a deep breath.

'Go on', insisted Billy.

'The police party caught up with him the next day at Pata Creek but he must have heard them coming over the rocky riverbed. He was ready for them. A gunfight followed, and Constable Clark received a grazing wound on the left shoulder. They chased him into the rocks but then they lost him. The troopers later said they were amazed how quickly a one-legged man could mount a horse and disappear between the boulders. Anyway, they patched up Constable Clark as best they could and continued the pursuit. Signs were rare among the rocks but the aboriginal tracker had listened to his father's advice and the lore of his people. He was an expert in his art; he always managed to find the path again.

They crossed and recrossed the creek many times but always rode upward towards the furthest ridge top, higher into the mountains. Until the trees and shrubs on the hillsides crowded into the creek bed and they had to lead their horses.'

Billy did not hear his mother put down his orange juice or take his bowl.

'They kept climbing ever higher until it seemed they could go no further. A wall of rock and wattle blocked their way. Then, on one side, Sergeant Bellows noticed that the creek disappeared around an ancient melaleuca tree that had fallen into the stream, the victim of a past violent storm. They checked further and found the trail going off at a sharp angle and disappearing into a narrow cleft that led into the hillside.

Some of the party were nervous about going any further, afraid that the bushranger would ambush them but Sergeant Bellows was determined to catch his man. He left Constable Clark and the tracker with the horses telling them to guard the track against any chance of their quarry doubling back and escaping, and then continued into the narrow cleft. Almost immediately, it grew very dark and Sgt. Bellows had to send the other trooper, Constable Gore, back for some lanterns from the packhorse. They continued and soon the sunlight disappeared entirely so that even with the lamplight, they could see very little beyond the slick walls and dripping ceiling of the cave. It was as quiet as a crypt except for the scraping of their boots on the rock. Then as they crossed a muddy patch, Sgt Bellows thought he heard a faint rattling sound from further ahead. The passage narrowed and they now had to squeeze in single file. Sgt Bellows was leading when the cave opened up on one side revealing a narrow ledge. Signs of boot marks could be seen on the rocks and in the mud, and empty food tins lay around, while the faint smell of wood smoke hung in the still air. He stopped in mid-step and held his lantern high. In its weak glow, a circle of stones and a half-burnt log confirmed that this was the bushranger's camping place but there was no sign of their man.'

Billy didn't hear his sister's protests or the comforting words of his mother as she released the child from her chair. He lent across the table, his face and mind demanding more.

'Where did he go, Dad?' he asked, almost screaming.

'Nobody knows, Billy,' his father replied in a low voice, 'there was no other entrance to the cave. They camped for the night at the mouth and searched deeper in but all they ever found was a single convict leg iron and a rotting wooden leg.

Legg, the bushranger was never heard of again.'

The kitchen was silent. The faint scent of fried butter hung in the air. A kookaburra called from the gums along the creek. Father and son faced each other with frowns and blank faces. The kookaburra finished its song before Billy drew breath.

'Aw, Dad!'

Boy's Work

Ahmed sank the bottle into the muddy puddle. Quickly! Others would take advantage of the lull. Brown water splashed as he closed the cap.

He straightened and scrambled to the top of the crater. A pit of broken dreams. The heavy bottle and loose rubble made climbing difficult. A shell exploded nearby showering him with dust.

He did not delay to thank his god but ran doubled, to the jagged row of masonry that offered scant protection. A shattered plank, once his school door, concealed entry to a dark sanctuary.

The water would satisfy thirst but not wash away despair.

Scapegoat

Marius Jackson wasn't his real name, not the one his parents had given him. It troubled him to think of that name, it belonged to another person, someone he barely remembered. It troubled him to hear it now.

The man facing him across the threshold held the screen door casually, his other hand curled behind him in the darkness. He was large and young and would probably be considered good looking were it not for the scar, which dragged the edge of his mouth into a lop-sided scowl. He wore a neat grey suit and blue tie. Marius compared his own worn carpet slippers to the other man's polished black shoes but came to no conclusion.

The young man spoke again, repeating Marius's birth name and adding a short sentence in a language Marius thought forgotten. That too sounded alien but Marius didn't need to reach back to his past to understand it. The tone was querulous; a demand from a life he thought was behind him.

'There's no one here by that name …,' he began, 'You ….'

'You can't hide forever Mr Jackson. It took us a while, but we know who you are. It would be easier for you and your family if you cooperate.' He paused.

Marius used the pause to observe and evaluate the situation. The shock of the confrontation was wearing off. In spite of the young man's words, he seemed to be alone.

'I don't understand. Who are you?' he demanded evenly. 'What do you want?'

'Someone you need to listen to, Mr Jackson. You need to come with us.'

'Rubbish, my name is Marius Jackson not ... not ... that other person. You've got the wrong Jackson. Try somewhere else.'

'Who is it, Mari?' A woman's voice, enquiring but relaxed, from the lounge room.

'I'll be there in a minute, Jen. Put it on Channel 2,' said Marius over his shoulder.

'Your wife, I think, Mr Jackson, Jenifer Reynolds, is it not? A linguist. A bright lady. You met at ANU. A chance meeting in your Russian language class, no?

'How ...?'

Marius tried to close the door and shut the stranger from his life. Before he could move, the younger man swung his right hand into the light revealing a strangely shaped pistol. Marius heard a sharp crackling sound before his body convulsed and refused to obey him. In pain, he felt his bladder release just as other figures emerged from the darkness.

'What a mess,' a female voice.

'Shut up and get him into the car.'

He was still twitching as the vehicle moved from the kerb and sped into the night.

'Sorry about the taser,' said the young man in a tone without regret. His voice echoed lightly in the room and in the morning light his scar stood out like dribbled porridge.

The voice seemed to come to Marius from somewhere far away. He shook his head to clear the lingering confusion and tried to sit up, reacting with a moment of panic to handcuffs securing his left wrist to a railing. A hospital bed neatly made up and tight across his legs. He flopped back on the pillow and looked around. The only other occupant of the room was his tormentor who sat awkwardly on a bentwood kitchen chair. With the exception of the bed, there was no other furniture.

'What have you done to my wife, my family?' said Marius his voice rising with anxiety and terror.

'We are not interested in your wife or your family, Marius. As long as you cooperate.'

'Me? I'm an old man. You know I can't tell you anything.' He struggled with the handcuffs in frustration and fear. The metal left vivid weals on his skin.

'Really, Mr Jackson, there is no point in struggling, you're not so old and don't take us for fools. We don't care about your secrets. The perception of truth is enough for us, and for the press. You're the son of a Chechen traitor who betrayed the motherland more than sixty years ago. That's why you're hiding in the suburbs. The press will believe this because that much is true.'

'Traitor! sixty years ago? I was a child!'

'Your father worked with Mrs Petrov at our embassy. He leaked information to Australian security. Surely, your mother has told you this? Your father betrayed his country.'

'My mother's dead. That's ancient history. I had nothing to do with it!'

'History? Did you know ASIO has watched you all these years? And we have watched them. History, like bad cabbage, has a way of repeating.' smiled the young man, clearly impressed with his humour.

'Your father was recalled to Russia with his family. Later he was arrested and shot, wasn't he? Your mother escaped from Russia with you. In Australia you grew up full of revenge, no? It will be easy to believe. Some will wonder why you settled down with a bright Aussie girl. More of your cover? Perhaps she is also a terrorist?' His voice expressed mock wonder.

'Garbage, no one will believe it!' Marius could think of nothing more to say. The young man regarded him, waiting for his further reaction.

'It must be difficult being a Muslim in a Christian country, Marius.' He finally offered.

'You clearly know nothing and believe in nothing. You are nothing.' Marius spoke with resigned passion. The young man smiled.

'I know this. You are from Chechnya, no? Tomorrow you will join your father in paradise, a martyr for Islam. But not before you commit a terrible crime and kill a lot of people including Sergey Lavrov. Oh, you didn't know our Foreign Minister was visiting? You really should read the papers.'

He continued to chuckle quietly as he reached under the bed.

'We found you some clothes while you slept, including this rather smart item. I'm sure you'll like it.' He flourished the clothing like a cheap tailor.

It took a moment for Marius to recognise what he was looking at. The most striking feature of the garment was the neat row of rectangular blocks that circled it at the waist. More blocks were fixed on what appeared to be the chest. Thin wires appeared to be threaded through the rough canvas.

'It ties up at the back,' said the young man enjoying the moment as he turned the vest around for a better view.

'Why, why are you doing this?' shrieked Marius, his eyes widened.

The young man did not reply at first. Then his false smile folded into a frown.

'Let's just say that my friends and I have a lot to gain from a Russian war with Chechnya. It will allow many other things to happen.'

'You're mad. This is Australia … I'll never wear that vest. You're wasting your time.'

'You will. Don't worry; we have drugs to ensure you do as you're told. But if you give us any trouble, we will kill your wife and family. You know the truth of this.' He leant forward spitting the last words into Marius's face.

'Here he comes now. See him, Marius? The one with the beard. That's your friend. Wait here and he'll come past. Get ready to shake his hand and give him a big hug. I have to arrange his luggage,' the young man patted Marius on the shoulder, turned quickly and disappeared into the crowd.

Marius turned back to the arrival doors as he was told. He felt hot and itchy in the heavy vest and linen coat and loosened a few buttons near his neck. His friend with the beard had not seen him yet, he was very close. People pressed, questions shouted.

Strange I can't remember his name. If only he'd turn this way, he might recognise me, thought Marius.

He pushed forward his hand outstretched.

Rather than parting for him, the crowd seemed to thicken. Strangers turned wordlessly and grasped his arms tightly. Held by many hands he was almost lifted off his feet.

'You can come with us now, Mr Jackson.' A male voice spoke quietly in a tone that couldn't be refused. He felt a familiar jab, and everything faded.

This time the hospital room was real. A thin tube hung from a stand and entered his arm above the wrist. There were no handcuffs and a small biscuit in a cellophane pack lay on a nearby tray with a glass of water.

'Sorry for knocking you out, Mr Jackson. It's policy. Struggling people are hard to handle.'

Marius could think of nothing to say.

'How did you know?' he finally asked.

'We've kept an eye on you for some time, Mr Jackson. Luckily your'e still of interest to ASIO.'

The man by the bed wore casual clothes but his grey hair was cut short and his brown jacket bulged in strange places. He smiled at Marius's puzzled expression.

'Perhaps you should have a word with your wife when you get home.'

He rose and moved towards the door.

'Say hello from Jim.'

Samantha

'Violets are red, roses are blue.' No …
'Roses are red, violets are blue…' Yes, that's it, how did the rest go?
Forgotten, like many things. Her mother would know. She pushed aside an errant trolley and moved further along the row of blooms. Something in a pot would last longer.

She selected one from the top shelf of the rack. An orange sticker shouted, *'Prices Are Down-Down'*, clashing with the bright crimson inflorescence that clustered like red cauliflower among the dull green leaves. Poinsettias seemed a bit early for Christmas but a popular choice in summer.

The girl at the checkout gave her the usual corporate smile and greeting but neither rose above her mouth. She seemed to have mastered a type of out-of-body state, leaving her body to move groceries while her mind roamed God knows where. Samantha didn't mind, she wasn't in the mood for pointless conversation.

She would need to change her clothes, of course. It wouldn't be right to visit her mother in her fluoro runners and Zumba leotard. Samantha suspected that the old lady would find the sight of a large group of women in tights exercising to music very confronting. As for shopping dressed like this …

I'm not my mother, she thought. She liked Zumba. It felt rather sensual to stretch and limber her body while her blonde ponytail whipped the air to the beat of *Nine to Five*. And yet, photos of her mother playing tennis in her younger days, all skimpy skirt, and fluffy drawers, suggested that they were not that far apart.

She turned the car onto the main road and headed towards the peninsula. Half an hour on the sand and then home, a quick salad and she would be on her way.

What to do about possums?

There were sure to be possums. Probably hundreds in such a place. Whole armies of ravenous possums roaming like locusts. Nibbling at anything soft and fresh. Tearing and smashing her precious gift ... Samantha checked her imagination, smiling at the lingering images. Still, possums were notorious for eating plants and flowers, weren't they? What if they attacked her bouquet? The old lady could not defend it. Samantha considered and dismissed several impractical ideas and was still battling with the problem as she turned her BMW into the car park at Bilgola beach.

Beaches have a way of slowing time, giving those who stop to listen, answers to many questions. On a day as perfect as this, the blue sky and soft warm breeze would speak to Samantha and she would listen. Provided, of course, that she could resist losing herself in a wave of hedonistic bliss.

The flags were in front of the club house and the break near perfect. Long rollers appeared to build on the horizon and gather in size before tripping on the hidden sand and tumbling to the shore. She had surfed this beach since childhood and it rarely disappointed.

She enjoyed a vigorous swim, caught a few waves, and lay on her towel for an hour. Nothing in this routine precluded consulting the gurus of the internet about her possum problem; after a few minutes, she put away her phone, showered and returned to her car. 'Poss-off' was needed and Bunning's would provide it. But first to prepare her salad lunch and change clothes. She would also need to spray the plant.

It was mid-afternoon before she left the house, replete with rocket, baby spinach, tomato, cheese, and mustard greens. The last had been a surprise grabbed from the supermarket shelf at the last minute on a whim. She hoped that the slacks and tee shirt would appeal to her mother. The poinsettia now dripped with enough 'Possoff' to resist a horde of the darling big-eyed beasts.

She stopped the car under the trees and followed the bitumen path to the lawn section. The pot grew heavier with every step, but it wasn't far.

The old lady lay near the lily pond under a large angophora. On summer days the tree shed its leaves in the breeze and dusted the top of the grave with a dull green glaze until finally absorbed into the warm gravel. The pot and flowers took their position at her mother's head beside the small brass marker.

The possum deterrent would only last a few days, but Samantha didn't worry. She could almost hear her mother saying,

'Thank you, darling. They're lovely, and my friends will love them too.'

Dark Nemesis

Billy arrived at the headmaster's office with five minutes to spare. He pushed back his blonde hair and straightened his tie. As an afterthought, he spat the 'gobstopper' into his handkerchief and pushed it into his pocket. The headmaster wouldn't approve of him sucking it during their talk. The hard round ball would last him the whole day if he didn't suck it too much so the short break would just make it last longer. It could always be retrieved later.

The sign on the frosted glass door simply read, *'Office'* but Billy was not deceived. This was the place to be avoided. This was the place where blind justice was dispensed. This was the place where his doubts and weaknesses would be exposed, his guilt displayed.

Facing the frosted glass, he drew a breath, twisted the knob, and entered quickly. The anteroom was empty. He released a sigh of relief, pushed aside a small pile of 'Our Community' magazines, and found a seat on the edge of a long wooden bench, the only place available. The bench faced two narrow windows shaped like hands clasped in prayer, but prayer would not save Billy today.

Waves of frustration, anger and guilt washed over him. He constructed dialogues of defence in his mind. He'd done nothing wrong, but this summons must have something to do with Wayne Harding's missing marbles. Wayne had made a big fuss when they couldn't be found. Two blue Aggies and a White China. He was a big-mouthed, blowhard, cry-baby, and Billy was the convenient scapegoat. He would tell Father Balkis. It was the truth. He would understand. Wouldn't he?

At a window, a pigeon fluttered briefly at the glass in a vain attempt to get a footing on the sloping sill. Finally, it dropped away with a flap of frustration and glided to join the small group on the quadrangle lawn. Billy watched it descend, returning to its flock.

Billy liked birds, not pigeons particularly, his father called them 'flying rats'. Billy preferred the big black ones like ravens, currawongs, and magpies. He liked their appearance of proud independence and apparent domination of the avian world. Nothing seemed to …

The inner door burst open with a harsh rattle, and a face appeared. A narrow, lined face with wire-framed glasses below a balding head and wisps of grey hair struggling to look relevant. A low voice demanded.

'Come in, Billy.'

His blissful solitude shattered; Billy did as he was told.

Father Balkis was a small, angular priest dressed entirely in black. He moved across the room and seated himself behind the largest desk that Billy had ever seen. His chair seemed to absorb him as he leant back, elbows on the armrests and regarded Billy with a frown.

Like a giant crow, observed Billy without moving his lips.

'What's this I hear about stolen marbles, Billy? That's not like you.' Billy wondered how the headmaster would know about him, fearful of his past behaviour. What had he done?

'I didn't, Sir. I couldn't, I was nowhere near Wayne's marbles! He's lost them somewhere and he's blaming me.' His voice rose, begging for belief but the priest wasn't listening. His frown deepened and he suddenly lent forward across the desk.

'How do you explain it then? You were the only boy around. You were both playing marbles, weren't you?'

'Yes, Sir.'

Father Balkis absorbed this confession without change of expression as he consulted a wrinkled scrap of paper.

'I'm told that two Aggies and a White China are missing.' He pronounced the names like two words from a foreign language. 'The China was a birthday present from his father, I'm told. If you return them now, I'm sure that I can get Mr Harding to forget the whole incident.' He punctuated the final words with an oily smile.

'But I didn't do it, Sir!' His voice rose again as he put one hand on the desktop. 'I don't know where they are or who stole them, but it wasn't me.' He felt his top lip beginning to flutter and drew a deep breath. His words hung in the air like motes of dust.

Silence.

Billy felt pinned to his chair by the two dark eyes from across the table. Surely his innocence was obvious. This couldn't be the end of it.

The dark face across the desk broke contact as the old priest rose to his feet.

'I must say, I am very disappointed, Billy. I thought more of you. I'll wait until lunch tomorrow. If the matter is not cleared up by then, I'll give you a note for your father.'

The walk home was the most miserable Billy could remember. The Gobstopper was no compensation, but he rolled it around his mouth, ignoring the furry taste. How could he prove his innocence? If he found the marbles, he would be accused of stealing them in the first place. The only solution was to find the thief but that seemed impossible. Where would he start?

He reached the park and set off along the shaded path that separated it from the school. Giant gums interspersed with casuarina and wattle crowded the park while over the chain wire fence, lofty pines and grevillea plantings edged the playground.

The scene had long since gone from Billy's sight, blinded by familiarity. What would his father say? His mother would cry, for sure, and his sister would think him a thief. How much worse could it get?

Suddenly a shadow and flutter of wings. Billy flinched as a crow, dark as night, swept past his right ear and stood before him on the path. It regarded him with a single yellow eye as though challenging him to take another step.

Would it attack? His father would know.

He dropped his school bag as noisily as possible. The bird took one step back and continued to watch him.

Billy regretted his hasty move, now he had nothing to defend himself. In desperation, he pulled the Gobstopper from his mouth and hurled it at the bird with as much force as he could. It struck the path an arms-length in front of the black apparition and lay in glaring contrast on the gravel. The crow cocked its head at the small white sphere. Billy stood unblinking. If he turned to run, would it attack? Maybe he could jump into the bushes before it got him? The crow moved, hopping a few steps, picked up the Gobstopper and spreading its wings, was almost in the treetops before Billy could react. He watched speechless as it disappeared among the trees in the schoolyard still holding the Gobstopper in its beak.

Seconds passed before Billy remembered to breathe again. He had a story to tell his father. He picked up his school bag and continued on the path, almost running now. He would tell everyone, he was sure this sort of thing had never happened to anyone else, ever. He slowed his steps.

He also knew who the marble thief was. Who would believe him.

Deep Secret

The thin line traced a silver arc against a cloudless sky and plonked into the water three rod-lengths from his tinnie. A frenzy of ripples circled the hapless prawn's entry and raced over the green surface towards the shore until lost among the mangroves.

Brian waited for the line to sink and gain tension, to telegraph to him the slightest nibble of the huge bream he was confident lurked somewhere below.

Patience and a clear mind, a relaxed body but ready trigger hand, that was all that was needed. It was simple, really. His mind filtered out the subtle impatient tugs of the smaller fish as they stole pinhead portions of the prawn. The bream he wanted would pick the bait up and drag it a hand spread away before a final furtive bite. Strike too early, and the hook would be plucked from its mouth.

Brian waited.

The sun was lower now, and the heat had gone from the day. He pushed his battered hat back to scratch his scalp. His short hair stood up like a brown wire brush.

The minutes dragged. Brian drew on the line a little to maintain the tension. Nothing, not even the light frantic tugs of useless smaller fish. A bit more, compensation for the wind and tide. The line didn't move. He dipped the rod and reeled in more line to keep it taut. The line resisted, straining against an invisible load.

'Damn, a snag.' he cursed internally.

He tried a stronger pull, careful to avoid the line's already low breaking limit. It might be a small mangrove branch or clump of seagrass, common enough hazards in the river.

Something moved.

A little light tension and he might just manage to lift the snag to the surface and disengage his hook. The vain hope of a flathead or crab had long departed.

Slowly he drew in against the load. Something large and dark began to emerge. The line was barely strong enough to resist the push of the slight breeze against the tinnie. Reaching for a boat hook, he groped for a hold on the unexpected mass.

He couldn't make out the hook or the sinker on what appeared to be something bound in rope. Dark seaweeds draped. Mud dripped. If he could find the end of his line, he could let the whole mess return to the river, but he didn't want to lose his hook and sinker.

Yet, something about his find made him curious. It was angular and half the length of his arm. The boathook had snagged a rope binding, and he pulled it towards him. The black mass now took the shape of a large box. A tradies toolbox perhaps but too distorted by seaweed and mud to be sure. He traced the line to the hook deeply embedded in the rope binding. At least he would save the sinker. As for the box, perhaps it contained something valuable?

He made a few more casts towards the mangroves while he waited for the sun to set behind the low hanging clouds then started the motor and puttered upstream against the tide. The small outboard towed the sodden mass behind the dinghy without effort as he hunkered in the stern. By the time he ground the small craft on the boat ramp in the gloom, he knew what he would do.

The box was probably light when empty, but it was full of water. Brian smiled to himself as he waded into the water to remove the motor and transfer it to his car; revelling in the opportunity to stretch cramped muscles after hours in the tinnie. He was enjoying this new event, an escape from boredom and now an opportunity for exercise.

While she lived, Megan had always admired his physical strength. She said it was a counterpoint to her slim and weak figure. As her weakness grew, he would pick her up and carry her on to the sunlit veranda where she could read and listen to the butcher birds warbling in the gums. That phase passed too quickly. He shook his head; five years of marriage and five of grief.

Not time enough.

He backed the small trailer down the ramp. The usual curious watchers had gone, and the carpark was deserted. Water lapped at the towbar of the car but finally, the trailer was submerged. He would sink the dinghy onto it. How hard could it be?

He thanked the weatherman for the warm weather as he struggled the waterlogged box over the transom into the sunken tinnie. He was pleased there were no witnesses but not worried; another fisherman would merely think him a clumsy novice.

His luck held as he inched his car forward up the ramp. Slowly the water-filled dinghy with the box in its belly rose out of the river. Water drained, gushing from the plugholes, and splashing noisily on the concrete ramp. He drove further forward, pulling the trailer and all it contained onto the road, still draining as it went.

Brian Edwards was confused. Imps of nervous guilt pecked at his left ear while he struggled to decide his next move. The cool glass in his hand provided no answers.

No one would doubt his right to the box, 'finders' keepers' was the code of the river. If the original owner should turn up, he might have a prior right, but Brian realised that he didn't want to find the owner if one existed.

He put down his glass and felt for his phone.

'Alec? It's Brian. I've got a problem.'

'Yeh, the last time I heard about your problems, I almost got killed!'

Memories of their first meeting arose in Brian's mind. He decided to push on and not be distracted by Alec's humour.

'Stop complaining and listen. I think I've got another mystery to brighten your boring policeman's life.'

'The only mystery is how you seem to run into trouble so often. Still, it's a bit quiet. What's it this time?'

Brian took a deep breath and prepared his story.

'I found something extraordinary while I was fishing this morning and I need your opinion.

'Bullshit, you've got into some sort of trouble, and you need my help. Out with it.'

'No, no it's a package, a box I found, I ...' Brian thought it better to cut through the banter and get to the core of his concern. He related the events of his fishing trip that morning.

'Do you think it's a body or something?'

'Not unless it's a child, I don't know, could be.'

'Where is it now?'

'It's draining in my garage.'

'OK, I've got a few things to clear up here before I leave. I'll come over about 7.00. You'd better have a few stubbies chilled.'

Detective Alec Lambert arrived after the news, laden with a six-pack, and still wearing his police clothes. The casual chinos and cotton jacket were supposed to allow him to blend-in. Alec knew he didn't fool anyone who mattered.

The box lay on the garage floor near the drain hole, its rusted and battered condition in sharp contrast to the immaculate workshop and bright lights. Alec hung his coat on a nail and turned towards it.

'I gave it a blast with the hose before you arrived but there's not much to see on the outside,' Brian muttered, pulling a short stool from under the bench.

The detective put his stubby on the floor to begin the examination. Something inside rattled as he turned the box over to look at the underside. After a few minutes, he placed it with the latch facing them and ran his hands over the rusty lid as though to divine the contents.

'It was probably galvanised and painted originally. No sign of any markings but it's very well made; factory-made probably. It looks familiar, somehow.'

Alec sat back, staring at the latch, then turned to Brian.

'Do you want to do the honours?'

Now the moment had come, Brian was unsure.

'Go ahead. It's probably nothing,' he said, recognising his preparation for disappointment.

It was a plain toggle latch but long rusted, Brian handed him a screwdriver and a hammer from the bench.

'You might need these.'

The thought that they could cut the hinges off occurred to Brian, but he hesitated. It seemed a pity to destroy something that had protected its secret at the bottom of the river, perhaps for years. He respected utility things, even tools. It wouldn't hurt to wait a little longer.

The latch yielded to the screwdriver after several minutes. Alec used both hands to pull the partly open lid back as the hinges protested noisily.

Silently they peered into the shadowy interior.

'Bring a light over,' he said, even as Brian moved to unclip an extension lamp from the workbench and hold it over the box.

In a corner, something poked through a sea of black sludge with metallic brilliance.

'What's that?' said Brian as he hesitated for a moment, then dipped in quickly probing into the black muck.

His searching fingers found something hard, and he pulled it out with a desperate tug.

Large chrome crescents separated by a short chain. Old style police handcuffs, swinging slowly, reflecting the bright light of the lamp onto the grey walls of the garage. Brian dropped the strange find onto the open lid of the box.

'What the devil?' Alec produced a torn rag, picked up the handcuffs, and tried to wipe away the remaining grime.

'Not worth much outside a museum,' said Brian, quieter now. He returned his attention to the box and thrust his hand into the sludge again, this time with more confidence. After a few seconds, he brought it out and dropped several small objects on the lid.

'Just a few old buttons and studs. Buttons, studs and handcuffs, not exactly treasure.' He started to reach in again.

'Stop. Get back. Don't touch anything else. I know what it is.' cried Alec, jumping to his feet.

'Bullshit …' began Brian with unusual eloquence, hesitating at the look on Alec's face.

'No, no. It… it will need to be examined by experts.,' His voice reflected surprise with undertones of anger.

'What …?'

'A policeman died. We'll have to reopen the case.'

Brian stared at him, open-mouthed. It wasn't turning out as he expected.

'I was just a young constable at the time.' Alec seemed to shake himself, his eyes fixed on something invisible to Brian.

'A jeweller's shop was raided in Sydney, Thursday, February 12, 1998.' he paused and shook his head, 'The jeweller used this tin box to take the best of his stock home each night for security. On this night the three crims waited until the shop had closed and the box was ready to go. Unknown to them, the jeweller triggered a silent alarm. A patrolling police car got the call, and two officers arrived.' He laid one hand on the box.

'One officer jumped from the car and challenged the criminals to give up. His courage didn't protect him, and he got a shotgun blast in the neck. He died instantly.'

Alec sighed again and took a long sip from his beer.

After a pause, he looked at Brian, his face distorted in a way Brian hadn't seen before.

'They got away with nearly a million dollars' worth of jewellery. A month later, we had a tip-off and caught up with two of them. We never caught the third, the ringleader, or found the box.' His voice dropped away as his mind searched old memories.

'Constable Jimmy Collins was buried with full honours. His partner received the Governor's commendation, though he didn't deserve it. The two criminals we caught claimed the third one was the boss and the one who fired the fatal shot. They each got twenty years, and life went on.' His voice finally drained away, and the garage was silent save for the creaking of the iron roof as the sunset.

'You were the other policeman, weren't you?' said Brian softly.

He twisted the top from another bottle and handed it to the sunken figure on the stool. Alec waved it away.

'Yes, I can still see Jimmy's face.' He was silent for a moment then pulled a mobile phone from an inside pocket.

'The two we caught told us everything, we think. The boss's name they gave was false, we had no clues to his identity, at all.'

He was already punching a rigid finger at the phone.

'Sorry, Brian, I have to get some people here.'

His garage would soon be the centre of attention, his find seemed more Pandora's box than pirate's treasure chest.

Brian groaned.

'Thanks, Ruf' The stocky man bent and picked up the newspaper that the old dog had dropped at his feet. He returned to his soft-boiled egg and toast.

'Is your mother out of bed yet?' the Labrador didn't answer but squatted patiently by the pool regarding his master closely. The water glittered in early light; a breeze from the harbour ruffled the tops of the pines below the house.

The scene reminded Craig Roach of a picture he had once seen of a villa overlooking Lake Como; the ornate balustrades and faux Roman urns were missing but the atmosphere of mindless wealth portrayed was almost palpable. He frowned; he had come so far but not reached those heights yet; he still had time. The children would both enter university next year and Peggy was pestering him to travel again. There was more to be done.

The man's long fingers finally defeated the cling plastic, and he spread *The Herald* open on the glass tabletop. He sipped his tea.

The economy wasn't improving, and cracks had been found in some aircraft, the paper informed him.

Idiots.

It wasn't until the second page that he noticed a small headline near the bottom.

'Fisherman's Catch. Lead in Police Death'

He put down his cup and continued to read. There wasn't much information but a spectre from the past had arrived at his table. Rufus stirred and whined weakly, as though he could feel the blood draining slowly from his master's face.

'The black sludge is apparently the ash from three pairs of grey overalls. Only the buttons and studs are left. Looks like they tried to burn anything connected to the robbery before they dumped the box in the river.' Alec read from several pages in an open file.

Inspector Schilling's office was large, and the certificates on the wall intended to impress but Alec had seen it all before.

'We'll get to that in a minute,' said Shilling, 'But first: Why am I reading about an ongoing investigation in the morning news, detective? The papers are making entirely fanciful speculations, and my phone has been ringing all morning. The mob in Sydney think we're bumpkins and if we're not careful they'll send someone to take over. You'd better get your finger out and get on top of this.'

Alec nodded without replying. He had heard similar speeches before and accepted the situation without rancour. His boss was a dim-witted pencil-pusher obsessed with the image he projected to his superiors. It was merely a weakness in the chain of command.

'We're following some leads on the box, the overalls and the handcuffs. But we're not expecting much.

'What help is that? Shilling's voice rose. 'We're at another dead end! Where now, genius?'

Alec paused,

'Well, it's twenty years since the robbery. When we first investigated, we had two hundred and twenty-eight suspects, according to the intelligence report. All of them knew the old jeweller's routine or had some other inside information. I think it is time to update the case file and see what turns up,' he paused. 'I'm also looking into another idea that might narrow things a little more.'

'You have a week. If you don't make an arrest by then, the case goes to Sydney. Get on with it.'

In the city, Craig Roach pushed back from the screen and ran a hand over his bald head. He had viewed every newspaper he could find and searched the internet, even the BBC had a short article on 'Fisherman's Mysterious Find'. Nothing new.

The police seemed confident of an early arrest. One paper reported that detectives had visited Ryan in prison, but he had said nothing, at least not to the press.

What was missing?

Fortunately, 'Sully' Sullivan had died in a prison bashing the year before, and Ryan was the only other robber and witness to the shooting. The old jeweller had passed away in 2005. Craig wasn't sorry Sullivan was dead, he was the smart one of the two.

Craig had taken every precaution; The others had never seen his face, and they hadn't met until the robbery, he used a false name and contacted them from a public phone. The stolen car was burnt and dumped, and the box sunk in the river. How could anyone link him to anything?

The email arrived in his inbox the next day.

'Hi, Craig,
That Sully sure was the smart one! Guess what I found in the box?
It's probably worth about $10k, don't you think?
   Involve anyone else, and consequences could be severe. I'll call.
Brian'

Roach pushed back his chair and stared at the screen. After several minutes his breathing slowed but the words remained. Blue italics on a white background. Perhaps it was a mistake? How had Edwards found him when the police couldn't? It had to be something from the box.

A brief search for the email's origin led to a server in Mexico. He wasn't surprised, it was what he would have done. He clicked on *White Pages* and began his search for a street address.

It all seemed so simple, but it took Craig another day to arrange a convincing cover story for his departure from his usual routine. In the end, he settled for a simple fishing weekend in the country. It wasn't unprecedented, and fishing was one of his passions. Brian Edwards would not expect him.

'I have a cunning plan,' stated Alec with mock mysterious tone.

'Oh, I like the sound of that,' replied Brian. 'Does it involve me?', knowing it would.

They sat in their favourite coffee shop by the river. Gulls soared in a light breeze or argued noisily for food scraps thrown by thoughtless tourists.

'We've reduced the number of suspects from two hundred and twenty-eight to only thirty-five,' Alec was grinning broadly. He didn't wait for a reply,

'It wasn't so hard, modern computers are very fast, and the software's smarter than in 1998. Some of the original suspects had died, some had gone bankrupt. If you have money, it's hard not to show it. The IT lads are very sharp. I am sure our boy is one of those thirty-five.'

Brian smiled at his friend's enthusiasm. He raised an eyebrow,

'It's still a lot of suspects.'

'Yes, well, that's the thing. He's like a lion in the jungle. We have to set a trap.'

'Tiger.'

'What?'

'Lions don't live in the jungle, tigers do. But I get the point. You want me to be the bait in your trap. Right?' He pushed his empty cup making a harsh scrapping noise on the tabletop.

'Yeh, It's not exactly legal but it's the only way. As soon as we find him, we zoom in and arrest him. I'm sure we will find the evidence once we know where to look.'

'God, Alec. That can't be legal. What does Schilling say about it?'

'Inspector Schilling knows nothing about it. It's all being done on my instructions, but no one will blab,' he leant forward and stared intently into Brian's face,

'You have to understand, Brian, Constable Jimmy Collins was very well-liked in the force. Some of the older officers are still in touch with his wife and family. He was one of us.'

Craig Roach was surprised by the size of the house, a spacious bungalow facing the street while the large rear garden overlooked the ocean across a coastal park and path. Holiday makers with time on their hands, shared the path with energetic local joggers seeking exercise and children on bicycles.

A brief computer search hadn't revealed much about Brian Edwards, it was a common enough name. He was obviously not the simple fisherman that Roach had assumed. It made no difference; he would be dead by morning.

There were still a few walkers on the cliff path when Roach approached the house that night. A light was on in the front, probably the lounge room. There was no light at the rear and the shrubbery in the garden cast dark moonlight shadows as he stepped casually over a low gate and followed a short path past BBQ equipment and under a low canopy.

Suddenly the yard lit up. It startled him for a moment, then he relaxed. If the light brought Edwards to the back door, even better. He bit his lip, unzipped his jacket, and moved his hand to the .38 revolver in his belt. The gun was licensed, his only problem had been finding cartridges that couldn't be traced. He finally took his chances and swapped a few rounds with old stock from the gun club armoury.

He knocked on the back door. The sound seemed to be absorbed into the timbers and diminished with distance. Perhaps Edwards was watching television. He knocked again, louder.

No sound but a new light, probably the kitchen. A male voice called harshly.

'Who... who is it? What do you want?'

A light came on over his head. He stepped back a pace and tightened his grip on the gun, loosening it in his belt.

'Just a neighbour, Mr Edwards, I saw someone in your yard.' He tried to keep his voice level. His throat was dry. He swallowed as he raised the gun and levelled it at the door. A loud click and the door began to swing inward. His finger tightened on the trigger.

'Don't move. You're under arrest!'

'Wha'! How…!' was all he could manage before a large hand clamped over his still-raised revolver and directed it upward. He tried to turn but was thrust roughly forward as his other arm was twisted behind him. A shout and the revolver was wrenched from his grip. He had time to glimpse Brian's amazed expression as he was forced to his knees in the doorway.

'Sorry, we were a bit late, Brian. We didn't expect him to go after you so quickly.'

'Yeh, well. I almost died when I saw him with the gun. 'Who is he?' asked Brian as he picked up his coffee cup.

'Craig Roach, the jeweller's nephew. Married, two children, has a place in Mosman. He's a jeweller himself, actually. That's how he was able to break up the stolen jewels, make new pieces and sell them slowly from his shop. He didn't need a fence,' Alec looked gravely across the lawn and the water beyond.

'What did Inspector Schilling say about the dummy messages?' asked Brian.

Alec chuckled,

'Yeh, there would be thirty-four very puzzled people out there. Most of them junked, deleted, or ignored their messages I'm told, but three tried to trace it. Roach was one. When we found he was heading this way, we knew we had our man,' he paused as a strawberry muffin was delivered and carefully cut into two halves.

'Inspector Schilling gave me a good dressing-down. I've never heard him so loud,' he paused. 'He's right, it could have been a disaster, but the arrest has made us look good at headquarters. His reports will be vague in certain areas, and I'm suspended for a week for not keeping him informed. He won't say much else, otherwise it will reflect on him.' Alec sipped at his coffee.

Brian smiled.

'I still don't understand how you got Roach to confess to the robbery and killing. If he'd kept quiet, it would only be attempted murder - of me.' Asked Brian in a puzzled tone.

Alec laughed,

'That's the crazy part. We searched his house. All the original jewellery was gone but we found a pair of handcuffs matching the ones in the box. A definite connection to the robbery; the ultimate *smoking gun*. We'll never know why the old jeweller had them, but Roach couldn't help keeping a souvenir.'

Cookies Anyone?

Cloe Witkowski had a disability. It wasn't a disability like her neighbour George with his blind eye, or her cousin Helen with her club foot, this disability was invisible. In fact, she was totally unaware of it herself. Her problem was that she didn't understand change. The subtle differences from one moment to the next as time interfered with the world and no two instances of reality were the same, these things were unknown to Cloe.

Nothing ever changed in Cloe's mind. Evolution was a contentious, perhaps religious, word; she couldn't quite get the concept. Growth was just something trees did. Cloe's world was made up of habits and patterns. The family home was one. The sun rose, the sun set. Work began at 9.0am and finished at 5.0pm; these were the patterns of Cloe's day. Imagination was not her strong point.

Most people didn't notice anything outwardly amiss in Cloe. Her work colleagues regarded her as a competent if somewhat dull accountant. The men she occasionally met liked her slim dark appearance and acted out their predictable patterns of seduction, mostly without success. She was a leader in her Tai Chi group. Outwardly, she was a pleasant, generous, if rather shy, young woman.

Unfortunately, the universe did not always support Cloe's vast library of patterns and habits. On one occasion, as she walked to the station to catch the 8.15am to the city, she found her path blocked. *Construction Work*, the sign said, *Please Use the Other Footpath*. Cloe was forced to modify her daily pattern. The abrupt change upset her whole day.

On another occasion Mr Reynolds, her boss, came to her desk as she prepared to start her day. Cloe had worked at Paterson & Reynold's for more than fifteen years. The firm provided inventory services to major industrial companies. It was her only job since leaving school, and she was now in a comfortable position. She didn't like to remember how difficult the climb had been. This day, Mr Reynolds came to her as she prepared to start the day. A colleague had called in ill, he said. He handed her a slim file and asked her to complete it before she left for the day. She tried to refuse. It was not her usual work

'It'll be easy,' he said.

'I have my regular clients,' she protested but there was no way out. That night she told her mother tearfully,

'He doesn't understand me.'

Her mother wondered whether anyone did.

Then one day, Cloe noticed for the first time that the basic patterns of her life had altered. Her sunny Australian world, once populated by middle-class, Anglo-Saxon people, had disappeared. Where once small houses and corner shops lined the main street, the view was now replaced by tall apartment buildings sitting cheek by jowl competing to block the panorama of fields and trees.

The wide footpaths of the shopping centre were now crowded with outdoor cafes and coffee shops that hindered her progress and smelled strange.

Her workplace too had transformed, expanded. Asian faces, once rare, were now widespread. Her colleague of three years, Dorothy, who usually sat across the aisle and exchanged smiles and nods, had left the firm.

Cloe had never met the large brown woman who replaced her.

Now aware, she began to look around with a growing feeling of concern. She saw her work computer, now two years old, as though for the first time. Was it her imagination, or were the other women getting younger? How long had Mr Reynolds had a grey moustache?

Her hands felt cold and clammy. Her pulse raced.

'Her name's Alica,' said Janet, who worked in personnel, as they sat together at morning tea.

'Why can't these jobs go to one of us?' asked Cloe, forgetting her own heritage, 'They always seem to favour these foreigners. Perhaps they'll work for less.'

'She's not really foreign. She was born in Bankstown. I've seen her file.' replied Janet carefully, torn between bigotry and friendship.

'Yeh but they're not like us,' offered Allen from Accounts sipping his tea, 'They have different values and habits.'

'Bullshit,' said Bruce from Packing. 'We're all looking for a steady income and a safe place to raise a family. My parents came from Queensland. I didn't wear shoes until I was eleven.'

Janet thought it best to change the subject.

'We were in Port Douglas for a couple of weeks last year. We swapped houses with a family Nigel met through his work.'

'Time I got back to the dungeon,' offered Allen, rising.

'Me too,' said Cloe as she followed Allen to the lift. 'See you at lunch.

'Hi, I'm Alica. Looks like we're workmates,' greeted the new woman from across the aisle the next morning.

'Oh, hi, I'm Cloe. Yes, Dorothy usually sits … sat there,' managed Cloe. Taking the large brown hand extended to her.

'Yes, I hope I can measure up to her standard. She seems to have been well liked.'

'Oh, yes, we miss her terribly. Er … er, have you done this work before?'

'Very similar, stock adjustment, inventory control. I worked at Herbert's for eight years until they went bust, before that in my father's restaurant. This is only my second real job.'

'Oh, that's terrible! I mean, losing your job. I … I don't know what I would do. New people – different work. It must be … terrible,' burst out Cloe. 'It would give me nightmares. I can't think of anything worse!'

'Oh, it's an opportunity to broaden my experience, learn new skills. Speaking of which, I'd better get to work. Talk to you later.' With a brief smile of perfect teeth, Alisa turned back to her console.

At 10.00am, Alica brought Cloe a cup of tea from the tea and coffee station, and they chatted at their desks. She lived with her parents too, she confided. It was not the ideal situation, but she enjoyed her mother's cooking.

'Have you ever tried *Kokis*? It's a Sri Lankan favourite. I'll bring some tomorrow to have with our tea.'

That night Cloe told her mother about all the strange things happenings at her office. The new people who were not like them but who seemed nice enough.

'Alica, she's from Sri Lanka, or at least her parents are. She's bringing something called '*Kohl..kies*', or something, to have with morning tea. I hope it's not too horrible.'

'It's nice that she's found a friend in a new office. The change must be difficult for her,' her mother smiled to cover her use of 'that' word. 'I'll cook some *Anzac* biscuits for you. You can take them for afternoon tea.'

The *Kokis* were unusual but very tasty, concluded Cloe the next day.

'It's from the Dutch language for 'cookies,' offered Alica.

Cloe wondered what the Dutch had to do with Sri Lanka but before she could ask Alica spoke again, pinning her with large dark eyes.

'Are there any decent men in the firm, Cloe?' she asked with a half-smile.

'Wow aren't you a surprise! Are you looking?' A reply did not come immediately as Alica took a short breath, her eyes downcast.

'No, not really, I suppose ….' Her broad face seemed to melt, and she dabbed the corners of her left eye with a tissue,

'I broke up with my boyfriend last week and I can't get it out of my mind.' She covered her face with both hands. Cloe could think of nothing to say. After a few seconds, Alica dropped her hands, forcing her lips into a thin smile.

'Had you known him for long?' asked Cloe to fill the awful silence.

'Four years and two months, I thought he was 'the one' but he seems to have other ideas.' Her voice rose slightly, and she drew herself closer, her eyes appealed for understanding.

'All men are bastards,' said Cleo, smiling to soften the cliché. Alica's smile acknowledged the attempt to change her mood. Cleo took her hand and looked into her eyes as they sat in silence.

A change had happened, Cloe could not describe it, but she felt more relaxed.

At lunchtime, she introduced Alica to the group in the lunchroom. Allen looked on sheepishly while the others plied her with polite questions. Cloe smiled to herself. The questions were not the ones that they really wanted to ask but those would come. Cloe realised that now. Friendship rose with familiarity and grew with time. People were not strangers one day and friends the next. The process was subtle and sometimes slow, but it always resulted in change.

The Grimm Report

(A radio play for three characters.)

Rodney Reynard: Overweight pompous radio host, nickname 'Foxy'.

Little Red Riding Hood: Naïve young girl with a penchant for the colour red.

Chuck the lumberjack: Muscular young woodcutter (lumberjack) and fitness freak.

Theme music: 'Peter and the Wolf', Sergei Prokofiev, (plays lightly on piano in background.)

General prompt: This is <u>ham radio</u> – act it!

Rodney (briskly)

'Good evening listeners, Rodney Reynard again, and tonight we at **Ham Radio** are delighted to bring you another interview in our series, **'The Grimm Report'**. Sitting here patiently with me today is the young lady at the centre of today's story, who simply wants to be known as **Little Red Riding Hood**.

Good evening miss …er…Miss… Hood.'

Little Red Riding Hood (LRRH) (timorous)

'Good evening, Rodney.'

(music louder, stops)

Rodney (briskly)

'Before we continue, I have to tell you, listeners. This story is one of the most disturbing I've ever heard in my 34 years of radio journalism. If you have any young children present, I suggest you send them to bed or turn

146

off your set. You can listen privately to our podcast on Thursdays from 10.15am on **Ham Radio 1777 FM**, as always.'

(music, soft)

'Yes, you may have already guessed, I am referring to the recent gruesome axe killing at Granny's House, as it is affectionately known. Those of you who are not locals will recognise it as the small cottage on the other side of the forest.'

Let's begin then, Ms Hood. May I call you 'Red', it could save some time?'

LRRH (resigned)

'Yeah, sure, Rodney. It's not my real name anyway.'

Rodney (brisk)

'OK, Red, let's begin. A wolf is dead, hacked to death in a bloody axe attack, we understand; what can you tell us about it? How were you involved?'

LRRH (painfull)

'Well, er, Rodney (sniffle), mum sent me to Grandma's house with some tarts and muffins she'd made. When I got there …'

Rodney (curtly)

'Sorry to interrupt, Red but can you tell us how you got to grandma's house. It's on the other side of the forest, isn't it? Our listeners want to know every detail.'

LRRH (enthusiastically)

'Yes, the path goes through those giant trees. Er, it's cold and gloomy in the morning but I walked quickly to keep warm, and I wore my red riding hood. Mum told me not to talk to anyone, but I did meet someone who turned out later ….

Rodney (interrupting)

'Just tell us what you thought at the time, Red.'

(music, ominous)

LRRH (cheerful)
'OK, Rod. On the way I met this tall hairy stranger with lots of teeth and bad breath, he walked funny too. He asked me what I had in the basket and I showed him the tarts and muffins. The cheeky fellow wanted one, but I told him I was taking them to grandma's house on the other side of the forest.'

(music, soft)

Rodney (impatient)
'And then ....'
LRRH
'Anyway Rodney, I kept walking to Grandma's. When I got there, I knocked on the door and a very gruff voice said, 'Come in dear.', so I went in.
Rodney (curiously)
'How was grandma?'
LRRH (worried)
'Well, she didn't seem herself at all. Almost unrecognisable!'
Rodney (rising)
'Oh, what do you mean? Were you in the wrong house?
LRRH (hastily)
'No, no. I was sure it was poor grandma, but she'd changed. Her voice was very deep, and she had big hairy hands.
Rodney
'Extraordinary! Did she say anything?

(music rising)

LRRH

'Only that her voice and hands could greet me and hug me easier. - That was a bit puzzling because grannie can be a bit of a dragon sometimes. So, I said,
'Oh, what big teeth you have,' and she said,
'The better to eat you with, my dear,' and then everything went black!

(music stops)

Rodney (busily)

'Amazing story, Red but I'm going to stop you there because I've just had the 'thumbs-up' from my producer in the control room. We have someone on the telephone who can add to the story.'

(Click ... click)

Rodney

'Hello, hello, this is Rodney Reynard. Are you the woodcutter? (pause)

Chuck

'Lumberjack!',

Rodney

'Yes, OK. What's your name, Sir?

Chuck

(pause) 'Chuck?'

Rodney (Signals to control room.)

'Of course, Chuck the Lumberjack. Just a second, Chuck you should be on-air now.'

Chuck (evenly)

'Can you hear me?'

Rodney

'Yes, Chuck that's fine. We can all hear you now. Please tell us what happened at Granny's House last week.'

Chuck

'Not much to tell, **Rod**.'

Rodney (irritated

'It's 'Rodney', Chuck!'

(music very quiet)

Chuck (casually)

'Er, yeah, sure. Anyway, I was in the forest and I decided to drop in on Granny.'

Rodney (puzzled)

'Was that something you did regularly, Chuck?'

Chuck (softly)

'Yeh, old Granny is well known to all the lumberjacks. She usually has a cup of tea, and scones or biscuits if we drop in.'

Rodney

'OK, Chuck, I won't interrupt again. Tell us what happened.'

(music louder, faster)

Chuck (evenly)

'Well, I knocked on the door, but Granny didn't call out like she usually does. All I heard was a very loud gulping, swallowing sound. I pushed the door open and there was this huge fat wolf about to climb out the window! When I say fat, I mean very fat, huge!'

'I said, 'Excuse me, Sir, should you be here? Where's Granny?'

With that, he lunged at me with his jaws wide open. All
fangs and foul breath!'

Rodney (surprise)

'Good lord!'

LRRH (horror)

'Gasp!'

Chuck (quickly)

'Fortunately, he was so fat he couldn't move very fast. I
jumped aside and swung at him with my axe.

I missed his head, but my axe split him down the
middle!

Imagine my surprise when Granny and a girl in a red
cape tumbled out!'

Rodney (curiously)

'Was the wolf dead?'

LRRH (delighted)

'My hero!'

Chuck (with sigh)

'Well, I imagine he wasn't feeling too good with his guts
split wide open, like that! Blood everywhere. It was a
terrible scene.'

(music soft fast)

Rodney (excited)

'What an incredible story!   Red, what do you
remember?'

LRRH (subdued)

'Everything went black, and then suddenly it was light
again, and there I was on the floor with granny!'

Rodney (brisk)

'What was the first thing you saw, Red? Describe the
scene.' |

LRRH (dreamily)

'Well, there was this big hairy wolf that looked dead on the floor and standing over it was this big beautiful (sigh) man in a chequered shirt carrying an axe. He had broad shoulders and legs like tree trunks. His blue eyes seemed to sparkle above his blonde beard and full red lips, I …. (breathless).'

Rodney (interrupting)

'Thank you Red, I think we have the picture.'

(music slow)

Rodney (briskly)

'Listeners, there you have it from the people involved. Thank you, Red Riding Hood and Chuck the Lumberjack. We're almost out of time, so I need to wrap up the Grimm Report for today.

We know that grandma is now fully recovered after a short convalescence at **Peppers Hunter Valley,** courtesy of **Ham Radio**, of course?

Under the circumstances, the authorities have decided not to charge Chuck the Lumberjack for killing wolves out of season, and it only leaves it to me to remind our younger viewers -.

Always follow your mother's advice and don't talk to strangers.

That was The Grimm Report!'

(Theme music)

About the Author

Chris Curtis grew up on the North Coast of New South Wales, Australia before he moved to the beautiful harbour city of Sydney and began a technical career. His early life took him to Europe for several years where he developed a life-long interest in travel and languages. He is now gainfully unemployed and writes short fiction stories.

He lives with his wife in Wollstonecraft, Sydney. When he can spare the time, he follows his other interests including fishing, gardening and caring for a hive of native bees. His published writings have appeared in Amazon eBooks, *Blue Crow* magazine; *Yellow Pearl* anthology; and *The Village Observer* magazine, as well as his first book, *Alfred's Tango, and Other Unlikely Tales,* published in 2019.

**